THE PHOENIX PROPHECY: ASHES

BOOK THREE

CARA CLARE

THE PHOENIX PROPHECY

When above turns to darkness
And below breaks free
A witch born to humans
Salvation shall bring
Fated to five who are not what they seem
The Phoenix will rise and become Earth's Queen
Into the embers
One
Two
Three
Devoured by Flame
The Phoenix is She

1

NICO

THIRY-SIX HOURS AGO

The older guy—the polar bear with eyes like crystalized amber—pours me a whiskey. He pushes the glass toward me. It scrapes loudly against the wooden surface of the table I'm sitting at.

We're in the kitchen of what looks like a mansion. Huge stone walls, old-fashioned windows, a fucking chandelier in the entrance hall.

The other guy is covered in congealed blood. He's leaning against the doorframe, looking out at an illuminated fountain. His muscles are taut, his shoulders moving slowly up and down as he breathes.

"Luther." The shifter puts his hand on his friend's shoulder and gives him a whiskey too.

"Is she okay?" Luther asks, lowering his voice as if he'd rather I wasn't in the room to hear the question. He has a shaved head and he's well over six-foot. Taller, broader, and angrier than me. A kind of heat radiates from him. Fire mage, if I had to guess.

"She's okay. Tanner and Kole will look after her." There's a hint of something in the shifter's voice… jealousy? Is that it? Not quite. More like longing.

I've been living my life as a charade for years; I'm adept at reading the thoughts people hide beneath the surface of their smiles or frowns or laughs. *Nico Varlac*; The celebrity. The do-gooder.

I shift in my seat. Thinking about the fire mage, the memory of Eve's flames—flaying my skin—sends a heavy jolt of nausea to my stomach.

My father said it wouldn't hurt. He lied.

As the shifter and the fire mage step outside, talking in hushed voices, I look at the birthmark on my wrist. More than the burns, it was the mark that convinced Nova I was her long-lost brother. Ironically, it's the one thing that wasn't false; I've had it for as long as I can remember. A blemish in the shape of a bird. I remember my mom kissing it when I was a cub, and I remember thinking it was neat that when I shifted it became a flash of white fur on my paw.

I down the whiskey in one then get up and pour another without asking. When the older guy returns, he extends his hand to shake mine.

"Mack," he says. "Sorry, we didn't have time for pleasantries in the car."

"Nico," I reply, smiling awkwardly because my head is spinning so hard I've forgotten how I'm supposed to be feeling. "I'm sorry," I say, looking at Luther as he ducks back into the room, bringing a wave of heat with him. "You're probably wondering who the hell I am."

"We know who you are," Luther says, sitting down, legs open, leaning forward on his knees as he nurses his whiskey.

I chuckle and swipe my fingers through my hair. It feels strange, laced with smoke. I need a shower. "I guess so. I'm on TV a fair bit, huh?"

"Nova says you're her brother." Luther ignores what I said about being on TV.

"And you called her your sister," Mack adds.

I nod. I'm gripping my glass tightly. My knuckles have whitened. Luther notices, so I relax my fingers and shrug. "Right. Sorry, I think maybe I'm in shock. This is all a bit…"

"Get some rest." Mack gestures to the kitchen table for me to sit back down. Clearly, they don't intend to offer me a room to sleep in. "We'll talk in the morning."

I swallow hard. Something about these two is putting me on edge. It's like they can see inside me; like they *know* I'm hiding something.

As I sit down, Luther purposefully takes something from his

pocket and places it on the sideboard. "I'm going to clean this asshole off me." He looks down at his blood-stained arms. Which asshole he's talking about, I have no idea.

When he leaves, I allow my eyes to focus on the sideboard. Shit. A badge. The fire mage is a cop.

When Luther returns, he and Mack sit opposite one another in silence. Exactly like cops. Cops guarding a suspect.

I close my eyes and lean back in my chair, slow my breathing, and listen. When their breath slows too, and I'm certain they're asleep, I sit up.

I wait.

I watch them.

If I'm going to escape, now's the time—before they start asking questions—because there's no way a wolf can take a polar bear in a fight. I've only met one in my life, and it's an experience I never intend to repeat.

I slide out of my chair, pull off my shoes, and leave them beneath the table as I tiptoe outside. Despite the cold, they've left the door open. Perhaps they thought the cool air would keep them awake. They must be more tired than they thought.

Just beyond the large kitchen windows, stone steps lead down to a large fountain. Beyond it, a cluster of pine trees.

I run, bare feet slick with the moisture of the cold grass. When I reach the trees, I stop. My heart is pounding so loudly that I can barely hear anything else, but I hear her.

Mother.

I weave through the trees. She's calling me. I follow her scent. I'm about to shift when something stops me. An invisible shield hits me smack in the middle of my chest. The air shivers. I try to move forward but it won't let me through. Like a pane of glass, the shield prevents me from leaving the grounds of the mansion.

They don't want you to leave. Mother's voice is in my head. I turn, searching for her, then see her pale eyes in the darkness.

She stops several feet in front of me. *I can't come closer. Spells. Powerful ones*, she says.

She sits back on her haunches and stares up at me, tilting her head. Her fur is pure white, except for the dark scar that cuts down the side of her nose to the corner of her mouth. Her tail flicks and curls around her feet. A growl rumbles in my chest when I see that it's singed.

Nova did that to you? I ask, the witch's name hot on my tongue.

Mother blinks at me. *No. The fire mage.*

I look back in the direction of the house. He hurt her. I should make him pay.

Nico...

I crouch in front of her. *Where's Eve? Can she get me out?*

Mother looks down at her paws. She licks her lips nervously. After a long moment, she meets my eyes. *Nico, Ragnor wishes for you to stay.*

"Stay?" My voice is too loud. She growls at me, so I whisper. "Stay? Why? What possible reason is there? He wanted to provoke her. It worked. You've seen what she is, what she can do. So get Eve, tell her to do her thing. Take the girl back. Kill her. Whatever. Just—"

Mother's snarl makes me stop talking. I lower my head.

We need time to regroup. While we do, you'll stay undercover. Tell us what's happening inside the house. Find out what spells they've used to defend this place. You'll be our eyes and ears. Her tone softens. *It won't be for long, Nico. We'll get you out soon. We just need time.*

Fear swells in my chest. I'm not cut out for this.

Schmoozing other celebrities, breaking bread with government officials, and feeding back the occasional secret is different. It's low risk. The way I prefer it.

It's no different from what you've been doing your whole life, Mother says sternly. *Watch, learn, report. That's all.*

I bite the inside of my cheek. "Watch. Report." I nod and stand up, straightening my shoulders, trying not to feel the grating of my burned skin against my shirt.

As if she senses it, Mother asks, *Does it hurt? What Eve did?*

"It's alright," I tell her.

She healed them, Mother adds, blinking slowly.

"Yes," I say. "She did."

I don't tell her that, while they might *look* healed, the scars on my torso are as raw and painful as you'd expect from burns that were inflicted just a few short hours ago.

You did well, Nico. Ragnor will be proud.

I look down at my wrist. At the bird. I try to smile but, somehow, the idea of making Ragnor proud doesn't feel quite the same as it did before.

2

NICO

TWELVE HOURS AGO

The next morning Nova appears shortly after sunrise. I feel her before I see her. Smell her too. Warm water, smoke, blood, and sex. As she enters the room, a wave of warmth comes with her. Like Luther's, but different. Her warmth quivers, moves the air, and penetrates my skin.

Her eyes find me and drink me in. She smiles. Her shining, silver hair hangs loose over her shoulders. She's wearing a thin white sweater. Black tattoo ink peeks through. A pattern that draws my eyes to her chest. I snap my eyes back to her face; I'm supposed to be her brother, for fuck's sake.

That's when I notice her eyes. One brown, one blue. They told me about it when they told me she used to have auburn hair, but last night her face was so full of fear and fury, and her eyes so dark, that I didn't see it.

My mouth is dry as I stand up and move to shake her boyfriend's hand; I assume he's her boyfriend because he's standing slightly behind her, taking up as much space as he can, shoulders pushed back, chest puffed out. And because he looks less than pleased to see me.

He's about my height, but more athletic. Floppy, light brown hair. California skin, like he's been sunbathing all summer.

"I'm sorry," I tell her. "This is odd. An intrusion."

Immediately, Nova pulls me to her. She holds me tight and close, as if she's been waiting to do this for too many years. I can feel her heart beating against mine. Her hands warm my back. Her fingertips smooth over my bumpy, charred skin and she inhales sharply. I close my eyes.

When she steps back, she takes my hand and moves toward the table. Before we sit down, she turns my wrist over and strokes it. She turns to the boyfriend. "Look. The birthmark."

He narrows his eyes, but nods. Straight off, I can tell he's an empath. He has the vibe. Luckily, I perfected my masking technique years ago. He can try, but he won't get any readings from me. No matter how hard he searches.

"Did you recognize Nova?" Mack asks, stalking over with a coffee pot. Luther is gone. He left while I was sleeping. The Viking—the huge, tattooed guy who got tossed around by Eve—hasn't appeared yet.

"Not at first, but now…" I say, smiling at Nova, meeting her sparkling eyes. "Now, I know exactly who she is." I take her hand across the table and squeeze it. A flutter of static tickles my palm.

"We have so much to catch up about," she says, her lips forming a delicious shape as she blows across the top of her coffee mug. "When did they take you? *How* did they take you? How did they even know about you? Should I call you Sam or Nico?"

Her face is bright and animated. An unexpected clot of laughter fills my chest. I'm about to tell her to call me Nico when Polar Daddy interrupts. In a tone that says, *I'm the big brother of the group and I'm in charge*, he tells Nova that he needs to debrief her. Learn all he can about what the League is doing.

Beneath the table, I catch myself tapping my foot and make an effort to stop.

Glancing at me, Nova turns to the boyfriend and asks, "Where's Kole?"

"Still sleeping," he replies. "How are your powers?"

Smiling a little, Nova opens her palm. A spark flutters to life. I'm watching it when the boyfriend says, "Nico? Why don't I show you around while Mack and Nova talk?"

I clear my throat. "I thought… breakfast?"

But the boyfriend isn't taking no for an answer. He wants me away from his woman. Away from whatever she's about to tell Mack.

"It's okay," she says, her fingers brushing my knuckles. "Go with Tanner. We'll talk this afternoon."

I stand and follow the boyfriend—Tanner—to the door. I pause before I reach the hallway. She's watching me leave. I turn back to her and, in my most sincere voice, say, "Nova? I'm glad I'm here. Even if it happened in a scary way, I'm glad we found each other again."

That makes her smile. She hugs her waist. "I'm glad too."

It's just past midday when Nova finds me. I'm sitting on the pool table in what looks like some kind of ballroom-turned-man-cave. Disco ball hanging from the ceiling. Sound system. Bar. Darts board.

Tanner's tour of the mansion lasted little more than fifteen minutes. The place is huge, and he showed me just a fraction of it. We walked past at least seven bedrooms before we reached one he told me I could take. Far away, I'd guess, from where Nova sleeps.

After a shower, I explored on my own. The ballroom, downstairs with a view of a tall brick wall and a winding section of a river, was behind one of the few unlocked doors.

And it's here that I've been waiting. For Nova.

I'm weighing a heavy ball up and down in my hand when she appears. "I found you," she says, smiling as if she's been waiting to say that to me her entire life. Walking over, she looks me up and down. "New clothes?"

"Tanner's." I look down at the slightly too-long jeans and white t-shirt he lent me.

"They look nice." Nova chews her lower lip. "Less… charred." She smiles briefly, then hesitates before saying, "Nico, if you want to leave…"

She doesn't know that her housemates—or whatever the hell they are—have locked me in here with their shielding spells.

"If you want to leave, I completely understand," she finishes.

I put the ball down. "Why would I want to leave when I've only just found you again?"

Nova tilts her head as if she's wondering whether I'm serious. "Because I put you in danger, and it wasn't the first time." She scans my upper body, searching for burns on my exposed lower arms. There are none; they're all on my torso. "I caused you pain once before."

I shake my head and gesture for her to sit down next to me. She perches on the pool table. As she sits down, her thigh brushes mine.

"You didn't kidnap me. That was, from what I can work out, the work of the Human Extinction League."

"Yes," she says, swinging her legs slowly back and forth.

I hold my breath, waiting for her to ask again how the League kidnapped me. Where they kept me. What they did with me before they dragged me out on stage. I've rehearsed my answers, but I'm hoping I don't have to use them; it's taking almost all the brainpower I've got to make sure I say the right thing while trying *not* to think about how fucking beautiful this girl is.

Because she is undeniably beautiful.

"As long as you want me here, I'm staying," I tell her firmly. "Although I have to admit, I'm confused about a lot of things."

Nova laughs. Her hair falls around her face. "Me too," she says.

Lowering my voice, I ask, "Why did they want to provoke you? The League? I know they're into some sketchy stuff, and don't get me started on their beliefs about humans, but why kidnap a witch? And the Viking? What did he do to deserve it?"

Twitching her nose from side to side, Nova chooses her words carefully. "It's complicated. But I'm not a witch. Not really."

"You can make fire with your hands, but you're not a witch?"

As she looks down at her fingers, a spark flutters from them. "H.E.L. thinks I'm part of a prophecy they're trying to prevent. It says a witch born to humans will stop the underworld rising." She twists her hands together in her lap. "I guess they're fans of it going ahead. So they were trying to figure out if I was the one they were looking for."

"A witch born to human parents?"

Nova nods.

"So, they used me to manipulate your emotions?"

"They knew seeing you would set off something inside me." With her eyes, she follows the spark across the room. "They were right."

I follow it too, trying to tie Nova's version of events together with what I was told by Ragnor. My head is spinning. Like I'm trying to keep too much inside it and none of it makes sense.

My whole life, I've believed unquestioningly that there will come a day when supers will take their natural place in the order of things. When humans will become our servants—or be exterminated if they cannot adapt.

My role was set in stone from the moment I was born. My father gave me up, denied my existence, and forced me apart from my mother so I could do the League's valuable work. So I could infiltrate high society. A wolf in sheep's clothing.

The rising of the underworld has been talked of for as long as I can remember. Ten years ago, members of the League started to whisper about a prophecy. Ragnor became obsessed with it. When the seer—Kole—unlocked it, everything shifted. Our entire focus was on finding the girl. The Phoenix.

Now here she is. Right in front of me. The one we've been looking for this whole time.

I take in her softness. Her curves. The blush in her cheeks, the deep pink of her lips. Her hair—silver like ashes—and the tattoo on her chest. Can it really be her? Can she really be the one who will end my father's plans?

Nova rests her head on my shoulder. For a long moment, we sit quietly. Finally, trying to remember I'm here to gather information, I say, "And these guys you're with; they're trying to protect you?"

She sits up. Something sparkles in her eyes as she thinks of them. "They are."

"And the floppy-haired surfer dude? He's your boyfriend, right?"

Nova nods and tucks her hair behind her ear. "He is," she replies, smiling.

"The others?"

She frowns questioningly at me.

"Papa Bear. The Viking. The fire mage."

A laugh tickles her throat. She shakes her head. "Excellent nicknames," she says.

I raise my eyebrows, waiting for her to explain exactly what the other three men mean to her.

"It's... complicated. Not with Luther. He can't stand me. But with Mack and Kole." She sucks in a deep breath. I feel like she's about to tell me more. But she stops herself.

Trying to lighten my tone, I shrug. "You say Luther can't stand you but, from where I'm sitting, all four of them give off serious over-protective vibes."

"They just don't know you yet, that's all." Nova nudges me with her elbow. The contact makes me flinch. I'm thinking about her. Her pale skin and shimmering hair. Large hands on her body. The Viking towering above her. Tanner kneeling in front of her.

I push the image from my mind. What the hell is happening to me? I'm usually good at this. I have very few talents but staying focused and distancing myself from the people I'm trying to deceive are two I can usually rely on.

"You don't know me either," I say quietly. "Not really."

Her fingers move to the birthmark on my wrist. She releases a small sigh. "I do, though." She looks at me and holds my gaze. "I've always known."

I frown at her. She's smart. Powerful. It shouldn't have been this easy to fool her.

Taking her hand back, she scoots away from me and folds her arms in front of her stomach. "I used to watch you on TV all the time."

I swallow hard. There's a sincerity in her voice that's unnerving me.

"I was drawn to you. I couldn't help it. Even though my boyfriend—my *ex*-boyfriend—hated supers. Even though it made him mad. I still wanted to watch you." She angles herself toward me. "I thought it was a crush. I mean, you're *Nico Varlac*. Everyone has a crush on you." She stops talking and frowns. "But I guess, if I did think of you that way, it would be kinda gross, wouldn't it?"

I'm still trying to interpret what she said about her ex-boyfriend. It made him mad when she watched me on TV? What kind of mad? My thoughts trip over one another. My heart thumps against my ribcage. "Gross?" I laugh and push my fingers through my hair. "No. I mean, we're not blood related. But what you were feeling," I paused, "it was probably just *familiarity*."

Nova's eyes graze my face. "You're probably right. We share a past." She unfolds her arms and reaches for my hand, slotting her fingers between mine. "We share memories. I've never had that before."

Looking into Nova's eyes, my stomach constricts. I stand up and brace my hands on the small of my back. It suddenly feels too hot in here. Too close. I point to the window. "Can we take a walk?"

Nova nods, hops down from the pool table, and leads the way to the front door. From there, we take the steps down to the gravel driveway and loop around to the back of the house. Stopping by the fountain, she leans forward and trails her finger in the water. Then she sits on the stone rim and looks up at me. "Do you remember them?"

I put my hands in my pockets and try to recall what Ragnor told me. "Not really."

"But you remember me?"

"Yes."

"Who told you I was dead?"

"I…"

"They told me at the hospital." She's speaking quickly now. Memories scratching at her throat. Desperate to connect with mine. "After the fire. But I didn't remember until Kole…" She trails off.

Mother told me about Kole, the Viking; a powerful seer who wormed his way into the League, then betrayed her. But I'm not supposed to know that.

Nova shakes her head. "Sorry," she says. "I'm still trying to untangle all of this. I'm not making much sense."

I step forward, close enough that I'm almost pressing against her knees. "We've got plenty of time. There's no rush."

Her eyes are watery. The moisture is making the blue look brighter, and the brown look darker. The contrast is striking. She sniffs, then tries to smile and says, "You know what my favorite show of yours was?"

I shake my head, color creeping up my throat. While I used to stick to speeches and charity events, recent years have seen a surge in high-profile reality TV appearances. Nearly all of them are excruciatingly embarrassing.

"*Voice Battle*. The time you sang against Brad Bennett." She's smiling wider now, her eyes dancing.

I tip my head back and laugh. That *was* a good show. I clear my throat and give her a snippet of the rock ballad I performed. "*When you're in my arms, I see nothing but…*"

"*Starrrrrrs*," she finishes, giggling. When she finally stops laughing at herself, she says, "Did you ever want to be a singer?"

I shake my head quickly. I've practiced this answer many, many times over the years. Every time a journalist tries to trick me into saying that, really, all I ever wanted was to be a celebrity and that my charity work is just a means to an end. "No. I guess I just always wanted to do something worthwhile, you know? Make a difference to people. I'm lucky I found a way to do that."

Nova nods. She looks impressed. People usually do. "You're brave," she says.

I blink at her. "Brave?"

She doesn't explain herself, just adds, "I've done nothing worthwhile or impressive my whole life."

"Now, I know that's not true. I saw what you did. You saved us from that witch. From the werewolves."

Nova presses her lips together. "Maybe. But I wasn't adopted into a nice family, Nico. A few weeks ago, my life was *not* a good one. I worked crappy shifts in a pharmacy. I barely had money to eat." Her fingers move to her chest. The place where the tattoo peeks through the fabric of her sweater. Once again, her eyes fill with tears. "I killed our parents, Sam."

I wince at the name. It doesn't feel right. "Please, call me Nico."

She doesn't answer me, just says, "Did you know that? Did you know I started the fire?" Tears are rolling down her cheeks now. Her shoulders start to shake. Looking at her makes my chest hurt. She's in pain. So much pain.

"It wasn't your fault." I dip my head, put my hands on her shoulders, forcing her to look at me. "I don't blame you, Nova. It wasn't your fault."

Nova holds my gaze. She's barely breathing. Finally, as my words sink in, her shoulders droop. She sighs and allows herself to lean forward, pressing her forehead to my chest. She breathes heavily, her back trembling.

"It wasn't your fault," I say again, softly. My arms are at my sides. My pulse is loud in my ears. I rest my hands on her back. She's *so* warm.

"Thank you," she breathes. "Thank you."

3

NOVA
PRESENT DAY

"Come away with me and I'll take care of you." Nico pulls me into his arms and holds me tight against his chest. "I'm your brother. I'll take care of you."

I'm trembling, but Nico feels calm. His heart isn't racing like mine. He's on the floor where Tanner threw him, sitting back on his heels. With his hands on my upper arms, he looks into my eyes as he waits for my answer. I hold the bedsheet tight around me. It feels strange to be so close to him when I'm wearing so little.

Behind me, the energy coming from Kole, Tanner, and Mack is making the air quiver. I look back at them. They're standing in a triad, each of them wearing nothing but their underwear, forming an arch around me.

Kole is clenching his fists. *Little Star*... His voice drips through me.

"Nova," Mack says, his tone measured but his eyes flashing orange. I can almost feel Snow pawing to be let loose. "We need to talk about what to do next." He turns his gaze to Nico, who still has hold of my arms. "Reacting on impulse isn't a good idea," he says purposefully.

Ignoring Mack completely, Nico moves his head and catches my eyes again. "Nova, I'm not sure you understand the gravity of this." He grips his phone and waves it at me. The video is playing on repeat. A gruesome loop. Again, and again, and again.

"You broke the treaty. The entire world was out for blood when they thought you *attempted* to break it. What will they do now they have video evidence of you eviscerating a human?"

I open my mouth to speak, but no sound comes out.

"He was a woman beater," Tanner spits. "He deserved worse than what Nova gave him. Trust me, if we'd got our hands on him first, we'd have broken the treaty too."

"But you didn't," Nico snaps. "*She* killed him. With magick." He sighs and shakes his head. "Supers and humans rarely agree on much, but they agree that a witch using her powers against a human is illegal. The worst of the worst. A crime so bad—"

"You're scaring her," Kole says darkly as a shudder runs through my body.

I shake my head. "You're telling me I'm the first super to kill a human? The very first one?"

"Of course not," Nico replies. "But you're the first to be caught on camera." He shrugs and waves his arms at his sides. "The Bureau has no option. They have to arrest you. If they don't, the FBI will." Again, Nico catches hold of my arms. Sternly, he adds, "Nova, I don't know what the deal is with you and these guys up here in this creepy old house, but it's pretty clear they can't protect you."

I frown at him. Heat rushes to my cheeks.

"You got captured by the League under their watch. They're not capable of keeping you safe."

"You fucking asshole—" Tanner lurches forward. Kole puts his arm in front of him.

Nico carries on talking. "Since you've been with them, *two* videos of you have been leaked to the press. The sheriff and his deputy got themselves fired. The Viking was kidnapped, and *you* had to rescue him. And don't get me started on Mr. Bondi Beach over there—" He cocks his head in Tanner's direction.

As Tanner strains against Kole, I jerk my arms free. "That's enough!" Fury swirls in my gut. Fire prickles my skin. Flames break out, licking my arms and fingers.

Nico falls back onto his ass and scrambles to the wall as if he thinks I'm about to do to him what I did to Johnny.

I don't want him to be afraid of me. I don't want to do anything that will remind him of what I did to our parents. But I can't let him say these things about the men who've risked everything for me.

I stand up, squashing the flames down despite the thundering pulse in my ears. All three guys move forward. Tanner's fingertips graze the small of my back. "Nico, listen to me carefully…" I hold his gaze and don't let go. "You don't speak about them like that. Ever. You got it?"

Nico blinks quickly. "Okay." He holds up his palms. "Okay. I'm just trying to look out for you." He pauses and tilts his head to the side, hugging his waist. "I'm sorry, Nova. It's just… I found you again. I don't want to lose you."

I breathe in slowly, close my eyes for a long moment, then help him to his feet with one hand while I continue to hold my sheet with the other. Then I push my fingers through my hair and sigh. He still looks nervous. "Nico, if we had twenty years of memories—birthdays, Christmases, family vacations—if we'd shared a childhood, and learned to fight and bicker and make up again, then maybe you'd be allowed to pass judgment." Over my shoulder, I can feel Tanner, Mack, and Kole. They're standing very still, watching me.

Turning back to Nico, I say quietly, "But we don't have that, and you haven't been here long enough to know them. You don't know what brought us together, you don't know how complicated this situation is, and you don't know me." I suck in my cheeks. "I spent years being told what to do, to say, and think." I close my eyes and allow Johnny's face to appear in my head. "I will never let that happen again."

"I wasn't—" Nico tries to speak, but I cut him off.

Snapping my eyes open, I step forward. "And don't *ever* tell me that my boyfriends don't have my best interests at heart because you have no idea what we've been through."

Nico hangs his head. He looks like a wounded puppy. He mumbles something that sounds a little like *I'm sorry*.

"I think maybe you should give us some space," Mack says, stepping around me to put a large, firm hand on Nico's shoulder. "We'll let you know when we've decided what to do about the video."

Looking past Mack, Nico seems as if he's waiting for me to agree.

"I'll come find you when we've talked," I say firmly, already gravitating toward Tanner and Kole.

Nico presses his lips together in a thin line, nods so that his floppy, jet-black hair falls over his face, then turns and leaves the room.

4

NOVA

When Nico's gone, I fold myself into Tanner's arms. He kisses my forehead, but he's still angry. His muscles are taut, his breath shallow. He strokes my bare back.

As Mack closes the bedroom door, and Tanner holds me tight, Kole sits down hard on the edge of the bed. He winces as he holds his ribs; still sore, despite Tanner's efforts.

Tanner chooses the armchair and pulls me onto his lap. For a moment, as Mack stands in front of us, his eyes trace the edges of the chair. He swallows forcefully and adjusts his stride as if he's trying to stop the memory of last night from tugging at his crotch.

"Luther was with you when you attacked Johnny?" he asks, skipping straight to business.

I nod, trying to focus on Mack's salt and pepper hair, and the tiny lines at the corners of his eyes, instead of the image that's pounding the inside of my head; Johnny's body exploding from the inside out.

"Then thank the moon he's not in the video with you."

"Small mercies," adds Kole.

I wait for Mack to continue. When he doesn't, I slot my fingers between Tanner's and squeeze his hand. "So, what now? Nico was wrong to try and make me leave. But he was right about one thing; this is bad. Very bad. Right?"

Mack rubs his neat beard, then stoops in front of me and kneels on the floor.

A smile tweaks my lips. "Role reversal?" I ask, nudging his naked knee with my bare foot.

Behind Mack, Kole's forehead twitches as he tries to work out what I'm talking about. To my surprise, Mack smiles and strokes the side of my foot.

"Are you blushing, Daddy?" I move my toes toward what I'm almost certain is a bulge in his black underwear.

He bites the inside of his cheek, then releases a sound that's half-laughter, half-groan. "Nova, now's really not the time…"

"Sorry." I shake my head, trying not to smile. "I'm sorry. It's just that you look really delicious down there on the floor."

"Then I better stand up." Mack swiftly rises to his feet.

His crotch is now at eye level. I raise my eyebrows, and say to his dick, "Not helping."

"I'm trying to tell you something," he says sternly.

"Sorry."

Mack reaches out and traces a long line from my shoulder to my elbow, skimming over the scar on my arm. "I'm trying to tell you that Nico was right. This situation—the video—it's dangerous. More dangerous than the last one. We might have to leave The Hollow. Go back to the cabin."

"The reinforcement spells. They won't protect us?" I ask, trying to picture what would happen if Bureau agents turned up and tried to break through.

Mack shakes his head. "No, they won't. If the Bureau wants you, they'll take you. So, pack your bags and be ready. I'll try the Bureau again, but I'm not holding out much hope."

As Tanner hugs my waist, Mack brushes his thumb over the tattoo on my chest. His white bedsheet is still wrapped around me, exposing the tops of my breasts and the pattern that Kole inked over Johnny's A.M.A. insignia. "Get some rest. Don't look at the news. I'll call Luther too, and get him back here."

"And Nico?" I ask. "Can you guys play nicely?" I turn to Tanner and give him my meanest stare.

After a long pause, Tanner sighs and says, "I'll go talk to him." He kisses my temple. Before standing up, he whispers, "Don't think I missed the part where you called us your boyfriends, by the way. Super-hot, Little Star. Super-hot." He nibbles my ear playfully. The steeliness that laced his muscles a little while ago seems to have dissolved. He's Tanner again. *My* Tanner.

I twitch my nose at him and, as he kisses me goodbye, I allow myself to run my fingers over his upper arms. "Thank you."

"I'll bring Nico up," he says. "So we can talk. *Nicely.*"

I smile as Tanner and Mack pull on some clothes then walk away.

They'll make it right with Nico. He said things he shouldn't have, but the guys have been on his case since he got here. Everyone just needs to—

"Nova—" Kole's voice interrupts my thoughts. "You're thinking out loud," he says, tapping the side of his head.

I blink at him. He smiles and looks down at his hands. They're pressed against his knees, as if he's still breathing through some level of pain. His boxers are black; most of what he wears is black. I'm tracing the hair on his chest, following it down his stomach to the waistband of his underwear when he looks up and says, "Nova…" As he speaks my name, a sigh that's almost a growl parts his lips. "Would you come here?"

"You're asking nicely?" I go to him and slip myself between his knees. "That's not like you."

Kole presses his palms to my back and draws me closer. To my surprise, he rests his head on my chest. He breathes in deeply, his beard scratching my skin.

I stroke his hair. It's tied back. I pull the elastic free and push my fingers through it as it falls around his face.

I missed you. Kole's voice vibrates inside me.

"I'm right here." I tilt his face up and toy with his beard. "I didn't go anywhere."

It's been too long since I was close to you. His hands are moving up my back. When they reach the sheet, tucked under my arms to hold it in place, they pause. "Let me see you," he says.

"You've seen me before." I lean closer.

"Not in daylight." Kole raises his hand and flicks it toward the plant on the windowsill. The small vine, which I thought he was going to use to throttle Nico, grows larger. It winds around the inner edge of the shutter and pulls it open.

Before, the room was lit by only the muted light from the open window in Mack's bathroom, bleeding gently through to the bedroom from the connecting door.

Now, daylight streams in beautifully.

My breath catches in my chest as the vine snakes along the floor and curls itself around the bottom of the sheet. With one tug, it falls to the floor.

My body stiffens.

It's so bright in here. Every inch of me is exposed. I have nowhere to hide, nothing to soften the swell of my hips or the dimpled skin on my thighs.

I cross my arms in front of my stomach, unsure whether to cover my middle or my breasts, but Kole's vine winds itself gently around my wrist and moves my hand down to my side.

"You're perfect," he says, drinking me in.

My core flutters.

"Every inch of you." He drops the vine to the floor and stands up. Then he turns me around and nudges me slowly to the mirror opposite the bed.

Standing behind me, more than a foot taller than I am, tattoos swirling over the cords of muscle in his arms and chest, Kole smooths his hands down my sides. He skims my hips, then moves them back to cup my ass.

"Do you see what I see?" he asks.

I hold my breath. A rush of heat flickers between my legs.

Kole's large hands, with their tattooed knuckles, traverse my stomach. They inch up and rim the sides of my breasts. When he reaches my throat, he fixes his eyes on mine, staring at me in the mirror, and flexes his fingers. Instead of gripping my neck, he draws a line with his thumb. He stops when he reaches the groove between my breasts. He still hasn't touched my nipples.

"Tanner and Nico will be back soon," I manage to say; barely audible because I'm dizzy with arousal.

"They'll have to wait." Kole spins me around. His tongue finds my lips and parts them gently. It caresses mine. I moan into his mouth.

He's about to stoop and pick me up, carry me to the bed, when I run my hand over the bruise on his side and say, "You're still in pain."

"I don't care." He rests his forehead on mine. His long, dark hair forms a curtain with mine. Ebony and silver.

"I do."

Kole looks back at the bed, then at me. He draws himself up, pushing back his shoulders. Trying to show me he's not afraid to hurt if it will make me feel good.

I slot my hand into his, move around him, tugging his arm. When we reach the bed, I hold up a finger, telling him to wait a moment. Then I arrange the pillows and nod for him to rest against them.

He lowers himself onto the bed.

I stand next to him. "What would you like me to do?" I ask, canting my head. "How can I help you feel better?"

Kole's lips part. He moistens them. "Are you wet?" he asks, his gaze flicking down to my pussy before returning to my face.

"Yes."

Still holding my stare, he tugs off his boxers. His cock springs free, but he doesn't touch it. "Come here."

Kole opens his arms and beckons me closer. I haven't seen him in daylight before either. He is beautiful. Utterly beautiful.

I climb onto the bed and swing my leg over so I'm hovering above him. His tip grazes my cunt. He reaches down and wraps his fist around his shaft, then slowly moves it back and forth over my clit. Desperate for more friction, I brace my hands on his shoulders and press down. When he winces, I stop, but he shakes his head.

"Don't worry about me," he says, letting go of his dick so he can lift my tits to his mouth. "Don't think about me." He flicks his tongue over my nipples, one at a time, then sucks hard.

I moan and press my hands to the back of his head, forcing his mouth onto me.

I need to be inside you. Kole looks up as he opens his mouth and laps harder.

I reach back, take hold of him, then slide slowly down the curve of his dick.

You're so warm. He holds onto me, his arms stretching up the length of my back, strong and thick. I feel small in his arms. Small and safe.

Kole sits back, leaning into the pillows. "I'm yours," he says, tilting his hips to an angle that makes me gasp. "All yours."

I sit up so far that he's barely inside me anymore. Then, gripping his hands and holding them up above his head, I slam back down.

As his eyes roll back and the muscles in his chest tighten, I clench my walls around him, squeezing hard as I move up and down. "Nova." Kole pulls his hands free and uses them to scrape my hair from my face. "Nova…" He says my name again, as if it's a prayer.

I lean back. He dips his head and plays my nipples with his tongue. At the same time, his hand slides between us and he toys with my clit.

The rhythm of his fingers matches the rhythm of his cock. I grip his thick thighs and grind forward. As an orgasm builds inside me, I pull his hand away from my clit. *Hold me. Close. I need you closer.*

He sits up, pressing his chest against mine as we rock together, back and forth. He trails kisses down my neck, tugs lightly on my hair, finds my mouth and groans into it as my core starts to pulse.

"Nova, I'm going to come." He sounds pained, as if he can barely hold it in.

"Wait." I rock harder. I can't breathe. I dig my nails into his back and cry out as my body explodes and implodes at the same time. "Now," I whisper, collapsing onto his chest.

Kole holds my hips, lifts me, then pulls me back down onto him. He swells inside me. Warmth fills me up. I clench hard, and he groans as I squeeze every last drop of cum from him.

For a long moment, we don't move or speak. We breathe in tandem. His chest rises and falls with mine. When he finally looks at me, he kisses my chest. The ink he left above my heart.

"Nova…"

I tilt my chin up toward him and kiss him softly, purposefully. "Kole…"

The sound of the door opening makes us both look up. "Seriously?" Tanner cocks his head at us, hands on his hips. "I leave you alone for five minutes—"

"More like fifteen," Kole remarks, not attempting to untangle himself from me, kissing my shoulder and deliberately grazing my skin with his teeth.

I'm laughing when a flash of movement behind Tanner makes me realize he's not alone. Nico's with him, and he's staring at me.

As he catches me noticing him, he clears his throat and looks away, shielding his eyes with his hand. "Let me know when you're dressed," he says.

But even though he's now turned away, waiting for Kole and me to clean ourselves up, I *know* he was looking. And I'm not sure how I feel about that.

5

LUTHER

I arrive at the diner just after sunrise. It's a twenty-four-hour kind of place. A box sitting on a square of earth next to the highway. Half-broken sign. Paint peeling off the door. Inside, I order coffee and wait.

I take out my phone and scribble notes:

- How did Sarah Borello find my number?

- If she knew Sam was alive, why didn't she tell Nova before?

- What made her pick up the phone and decide to finally divulge her secret?

Three times, as the clock ticks on, the waitress asks if I want food. Eventually, I give in and order waffles with bacon; might as well eat if I'm here.

While I wait for the waffles to arrive, I search for information about Sarah Borello. She's on all the usual social media sites, but with locked-down profiles and the same profile picture on each.

I type in *Sarah Borello, Ridgemore,* and an address listing comes up. The same apartment block as Nova; so, she wasn't lying about that, at least.

No job info, though she sounded old enough to be retired, so that doesn't surprise me. Human and magick police forces have an agreement that they'll share information when requested, but a request would take too long. So, I'll have to make do with knowing her name and the fact she lives in Ridgemore.

At the same moment the waffles arrive, my cell rings. It's Mack.

"Everything okay?" I ask, shoveling food into my mouth.

"Where are you?" Mack's tone is off. Urgent.

I put down my fork and lean forward onto the table. "Following a lead about Nico."

There's a pause. Mack breathes out sharply. "You haven't seen the news?"

"No, why?" I wrap my fingers around my mug and heat the now-lukewarm coffee inside.

"Someone released video footage from the stairwell. Nova... and Johnny."

My grip tightens on the mug. The liquid inside starts to bubble.

"You're not in it," Mack says hurriedly. "I'm trying to get through to the Bureau now, but we're preparing to leave. Can you get back here?"

I look at my watch. It's only seven a.m., which means I have an hour to wait. "I can't leave yet. Give me three hours."

"Three?"

"It's important, boss." I pinch the bridge of my nose. "If I can't make it back in time, and you need to leave, pack me a bag. I'll meet you at the cabin."

"Alright."

Before he hangs up, I add, "Mack?"

"Yeah?"

"Don't leave Nico alone with Nova."

Mack pauses as if he's about to ask me to elaborate but has realized we don't have time. "I'll make sure of it," he says, then puts down the phone.

When Sarah arrives, I recognize her instantly from the pictures online. Gray hair, pale eyes, pale skin, and wrapped in a knitted forest green cardigan.

Her eyes lock onto me, and she hurries over, clutching the cardigan in front of her. When she reaches me, she slides into the seat opposite me and looks over her shoulder. She couldn't be more obviously trying not to be noticed if she had a sign reading, *Don't follow me,* on her back.

"Sergeant Ross?"

"Deputy," I correct her. "But you can call me Luther."

"Luther." She nods and looks at my coffee. I wave for the server to bring us another mug. "I'm Sarah."

I fold my arms and sit back. She has a plain face. Unremarkable. No makeup, slim, deep lines at the corners of her eyes.

"How is Nova?" she asks quietly. "I saw the news. She must be terrified." She lets go of the cardigan and wrings her hands together. She's wearing a silver cross around her neck. "After everything Johnny put her through, how anyone could think he didn't deserve it..." She trails off. "Is she alright?" She repeats her question.

Unfolding my arms, I lean forward. "How about before I answer your questions, you answer mine?"

Sarah blinks several times, then nods. "Of course."

"First, why did you contact me? How did you know I was connected to Nova?"

Sarah's eyes dart over to the server, who's finally bringing the mug. When it arrives, she pours a large cup and adds three spoonsful of sugar. She takes a long drink before answering me. "I came to Phoenix Falls to find Nova. To check she was okay."

I narrow my eyes. "Nova didn't say anything about seeing you."

"That's because she didn't. I saw her walk into a bar. The Solar Cross. I followed her in and saw she was serving. She looked… happy. You were there talking to her. You dropped a business card. So, I picked it up. Just in case."

"I dropped a business card? That sounds unlikely."

She swallows hard and looks down into her drink. Tilting her head from side to side, she says, "It was sticking out of your pocket. I might have…" She taps her long fingernails on the side of the mug, then looks up at me. "I'm a witch," she says firmly, sitting up a little straighter. "When I saw the card sticking out of your pocket—"

"You *made* me drop it?"

She dips her head. "Yes."

I fold my arms again. We've been talking for less than five minutes, and she's lied already. "You don't feel like a witch," I say, searching for an aura and finding nothing. "You feel human."

"I'm un-elemental," she says, her lips tightening. "I have no affinity."

"I know what it means." Un-elemental witches are rare, and generally looked on with suspicion by other supers.

Sarah starts to fiddle with a button on her cardigan.

"Alright," I say. "So we know *how* you found me. Now tell me *why*. Why call? Why now? With all that's going on, what makes you think Nova needed to know about her brother when you've kept his existence to yourself all these years?"

Flattening her palms on the table, Sarah breathes out slowly. "In order to tell you that, I need to tell you all of it," she says, glancing over her shoulder to check that we're still alone.

"I have time." I pick up my cell and press record on the voice recording app. "Whenever you're ready."

Sarah looks at the phone. Hesitantly, she begins. "Twenty-four years ago, I was working as a midwife. I was on a night shift. It was late; nearly midnight. It was raining. The kind of rain where you can barely see your hand in front of your face." Sarah closes her eyes as she remembers. "A young mother was brought in. She was twenty-one. Human. Her husband was older than her, and he was a werewolf.

"The husband was terrified. He was making such a fuss that I told him to wait outside. The mother... her name was Elena. She was beautiful. Jet-black hair, wide eyes. Mesmerizing, and very sweet. She told me that their marriage, and the pregnancy, had happened quickly. Neither of their families were happy, but they were over the moon." Sarah draws in a deep breath. "However, she was only thirty-six weeks along. The baby was early." Sarah looks down at her fingernails. "There were complications. The baby came. He was small, but perfect. A beautiful little boy.

Then Elena started bleeding. Too much blood." Sarah looks up at me. "We couldn't save her."

"The baby was Sam?" I ask, keeping my voice low, glancing at my phone to make sure it's still recording.

Sarah nods slowly. "Yes, the baby was Sam."

6

MACK

"Fuck!" I slam the phone down. Instantly, Snow breaks through. I let it happen; feel my muscles stretch and my bones crack. Pain and pleasure merge. Power shakes through me as I grow bigger and stronger, and thoughts give way to urges.

I rarely shift in the house. Let alone my study. There's hardly room for us here. Snow swipes our paw over the desk, knocks the phone flying, opens our mouth, and roars at the ceiling.

The light fitting rattles.

"Mack?" We hear her before we see her.

When we turn around, there she is. In the doorway. She sees us and her eyes widen. They roam our white fur, take in the shape of our shoulders, our thick powerful legs, our heavy feet.

"Snow..." she whispers.

His name on her lips makes Snow open our mouth and pant.

"It's nice to see you again." She weaves her fingers into our fur. "But I could kinda use Mack right now."

At that, Snow huffs hard. I laugh and he huffs louder.

As I turn back into myself, Nova stays very still. She watches the transformation without looking away. When I'm me again, standing butt-naked in front of her, she breathes, "Wow. That was…"

The shape of her lips when they say *wow* makes my cock twitch. As if she can tell, she looks purposefully down and raises an eyebrow.

"Impressive?" I ask, surprised that I'm letting myself flirt with her. Especially now when there are a million other things that are more important than hormones to deal with.

"Very impressive." She moves forward. Her fingernail grazes my thigh. I close my eyes, but then shake my head and step away from her.

"That's not what you needed me for," I say as I take fresh clothes from my desk drawer, pull them on, and sit down.

Perching on the desk, Nova says, "No. It isn't."

I wait for her to elaborate.

"I heard you yelling. I thought maybe you had news… from the Bureau?" She takes her cell from her pocket and places it firmly on the desk. "I kind of ignored your advice to stay away from the internet." She meets my eyes. Her expression has changed. The flirty sparkle has gone, replaced with worry. "They're saying some pretty scary things about me, Mack."

I hate having to tell her I failed her. I rub my knees beneath the desk and sigh. "I'm sorry." I shake my head as I look up at her. "They won't budge. Wouldn't even hear me out."

Immediately, Nova jumps down and walks to my side of the desk. She nudges my chair so it swivels around so she can slide onto my lap.

"You tried, Daddy," she whispers, leaning down to kiss the spot below my ear.

I sit stiffly beneath her, unsure of what to do. I gave in last night, but I hadn't thought about what it meant. Except that it's filled me with feelings I haven't visited in years. Nova, however, seems to have decided for herself. She puts one hand firmly on my chest and slots her other fingers between mine.

"I worked with them for twenty-five years, and it means nothing." In my head, Snow paces back and forth; he's as pissed as I am.

"Don't they have files?" she asks. "Records of what you did for them?"

A wry smile parts my lips. "Yes, they do. Which is part of the problem."

Nova frowns at me.

Finally, I allow myself to wrap my arm free around her waist.

Her sweater has ridden up. My fingers graze a small patch of bare skin above her hip. It's soft and smooth. She breathes in and smiles as I stroke it with my thumb. "I joined the Bureau straight out of college. I was recruited, like Luther. Worked my way up through the ranks. But almost everyone who was there when I left to teach has gone now. And if all they have is my file to go by…" I look down at our entwined fingers. For a moment, I can't distinguish hers from mine.

"Your file says not-so-good things?"

I nod solemnly. "When Kole was undercover, our objective was to gather information about the League. Our primary goal was to identify their leader. Second to that, to pass on details of any planned terrorist activity so the Bureau could put a stop to it." I move my hand from her side to her thigh, smoothing my palm over her jeans. "When Kole revealed the League was trying to access a prophecy, the Bureau categorically told him *not* to get involved. They said that if he couldn't maintain his cover while distancing himself from it, then he should be extricated."

"But he didn't leave…" Nova says, her brow creasing as she tries to recall what she knows about Kole's time undercover.

"No. He stayed. He believed the prophecy was important, and that if he didn't access it and pass them false information, they'd find another seer. One who would simply hand it over. Luther and I agreed with him. So—"

"So, you went against your orders?"

"We told our superiors that Kole was working on other leads. In fact, for the three years he was there, he was focused almost entirely on the prophecy."

"You went against orders for three years," Nova says, her eyebrow arching.

"Yes, which would have been fine if it all went to plan. But when Kole failed to withhold the prophecy from Kayla, and we had to pull him out…" I pinch the bridge of my nose. I try not to think of those days. The days after. With Kole gone, and Luther and I left trying to salvage our careers. "We tried to convince them to take The Phoenix Prophecy seriously," I say darkly. "They didn't believe us. At least, they didn't believe in its gravity." I laugh a little and shake my head. "They said they'd pass it to the Prophecies and Scrolls Department."

"There's a department for that?" Nova smiles with the corner of her mouth.

"There's a department for pretty much everything." I inhale deeply and rub the spot between her shoulders. "Luther and I walked away. We trusted Kole, and he believed—still does—that The Phoenix Prophecy has the potential to save the world. That if the prophecy is prevented from happening—if The Phoenix is stopped—life as we know it will end."

Nova shudders and I pull her closer. "So, in summary, your file says, 'Naughty Mack', and anyone who reads it will think you're not to be trusted."

I reach up and tuck her hair behind her ear. "I'm sorry, Nova. I tried. But I think it's time to—"

A thunderous banging on the door makes me stop talking. "Mack? Nova?"

"Tanner?" Nova hops down from my lap and goes to open the door. When Tanner enters, his eyes skim over me like he's checking I'm fully clothed.

"We have a situation." He crosses the room in just a few strides and peers out through the window.

"The shields? Are they down?" I push my chair back and spring to my feet.

"No. They're holding." Tanner turns around and looks from me to Nova. "But I'm not sure for how long." He reaches into his pocket and takes out his cell. When he passes it to me, I hold it so Nova can see.

"Is that…?"

"News crews. In the woods. Filming. Trying to break through." Tanner turns to the window again.

Nova's face pales. She reaches for my hand and squeezes it tight.

Passing the phone back to Tanner, I turn on the TV above the fireplace. Every news channel shows the same thing; hordes of reporters lining the shield in the woods. As Tanner stands on the other side of Nova and takes her other hand, the footage changes to an aerial view of a line of black SUVs. Next, a chopper.

"A fucking chopper?" Tanner's mouth drops open. He shakes his head. "Turn it off, Mack."

I ignore him. Turning back to the desk, I pick up my cell and redial. It rings twice.

"Tom? Don't hang up."

There's a long pause. "Sheriff, the last time we spoke—which was about ten minutes ago—you cursed at me and hung up."

"I know. I know. But listen… please. I need you to listen." This time, I'm begging. I'm not trying to sound important or experienced. I'm not using my 'agent' voice. I am quite literally begging him to listen to me.

Agent Tom Haze exhales loudly. "You have ten seconds."

"Annalise McCourt," I speak quickly. "I'm not asking to speak to her. I'm not asking you to put me through. But I know *you* can talk to her if it's an emergency. This is an emergency, Tom. If we play this wrong, it will have dire consequences."

"Are you threatening me, Sheriff?"

"No. Of course, not. But there's more at stake than you realize." I pause and look at Nova. She's watching me, still holding Tanner's hand. "Speak to Annalise. Ask her if I can be trusted. If she says yes, call off the chopper and the SUVs, and come here yourself. Just you. We'll talk. I'll explain everything. I'll explain why Nova is *not* a threat. She'll tell you herself."

Tom Haze doesn't reply. The line goes dead.

7

LUTHER

"After he was born, Sam needed to stay in the hospital for a while. We kept him for three weeks." Sarah bites her lower lip. "His father didn't visit him once. He was just too heartbroken." A note of pride laces her voice as she adds, "But I did. I stayed with him. Every day, every night. I took care of him.

"Finally, his father returned. But he could barely look at the baby. He went away again and, the next time he came, he asked how much he would have to pay me to be Sam's nanny— to go home with them, live in his house, and take care of the baby." Sarah reaches into her purse and takes out a stack of photographs. She pushes them over to me. Images of a baby boy swaddled in a crib. Images of a younger Sarah holding the same baby, smiling as if she's his mother.

"He agreed to match my salary from the hospital, so off we went." She looks down at the photos and traces her finger over one of them. "For three years, we were happy. Me and Sam in our own little world.

"His father had a huge old house on the outskirts of Solleville. He gave us a wing all to ourselves. Just Sam and I." She smiles. It's a smile filled with sadness and nostalgia. Then her face drops. "As Sam got older, I found it harder to keep him away from his father. He wanted to know him. Wanted to be around him. But his father was still too broken. When he looked at Sam, he saw Elena."

Sarah shuffles the pictures and shows me another. Sam as a toddler, standing between a couple in their fifties.

"Just after Sam's third birthday, Elena's parents found us. They told his father they wanted custody." Her eyes widen and she shakes her head. "I expected him to fight, but he didn't even try. He agreed they should adopt Sam. He relinquished custody to them and told me to leave."

I lace my fingers together. "If his grandparents adopted him, how did he end up with Nova's parents?" I'm trying to figure out how a werewolf cub ended up being fostered in Ridgemore; the most anti-magick town in the state.

"On Sam's *fourth* birthday—"

Suddenly, the pieces drop. "Werewolves start to shift when they're four years old," I mutter, filling in the blank.

Sarah nods. "They thought they could handle it, but they

couldn't. They tried to return him to his father. But in the time Sam had been gone, his father had gotten caught up with the Human Extinction League. He'd come to believe that Elena died because she was weak. He loved her but *hated* her for leaving him, and that hatred spread to *all* humans."

"And hybrids," I add. "Like his son."

"Yes." Sarah takes a long sip of coffee. "At the time, Supernatural Child Services were trying to forge links with the human foster system. They were running a program to place supers with humans. Nova's parents had signed up."

"And they got Sam…"

"They got Sam," Sarah repeats.

"Where were you at this point? What did you do when you left the house?"

Sarah moistens her lips and sighs. "I'd been working as a temp nurse in Solleville. Saving money. I planned to fight Sam's grandparents for custody. When he was placed with Nova's parents, I moved to Ridgemore so I could stay close to him. But when I met them—Alice and Charles—and I saw how happy Sam was…" Tears filled Sarah's eyes. She wipes them with the back of her hand then selects another photograph and hands it to me.

I study it carefully. A woman with vivid auburn hair, a man with a dark brown beard and small round glasses. Between them, a small girl. Five or six years old. Auburn hair in bunches tied with pink bows. She's staring at a boy. Sam. Wrinkling her nose at him while he grins a gap-toothed grin back at her.

"I decided that maybe just staying close to him would be enough," Sarah says as she tilts her head at the picture. "They were so happy for such a short time."

I put the photograph down and add it back to the pile. "You were in Ridgemore when Nova's parents died?"

"I was living across the street in a small apartment. I often saw the kids playing outside. Alice and Charles had both taken time off work to help Sam settle, but I planned to introduce myself when they got back into their routine. Offer to babysit..." She stops and shakes her head as memories of what could have been dance in front of her eyes. "The night of the fire, I was coming back from work. I saw the smoke. Heard sirens in the distance. All the neighbors were standing there, just watching. But I ran inside. I found Sam passed out near the door. I grabbed him and carried him out to the sidewalk. I was about to go back for Nova when she appeared. From nowhere. From the flames."

"Without a mark on her?" I ask, even though I already know the answer.

"Not even first-degree burns." Sarah sits back and folds her arms in front of her chest, hugging herself as if she's suddenly chilled. "She was taken to a human hospital. Sam was in the same ambulance, but when they realized he was a wolf cub, they called a supernatural facility nearby."

"You went with Sam?"

Sarah nods. "I called his father and told him what had happened. I truly expected him to come, but he didn't even return my call. The next day, Supernatural Child Services turned up and took him away. I pleaded with them not to. I begged them, but they didn't listen."

"And Nova?" I swallow hard, my chest flickering with heat as I picture her. So small, and all alone.

"She was placed with a foster family in Ridgemore." Sarah is staring at the photograph of Sam and Nova together. "I tried to find out where Sam was. They wouldn't tell me, but they let me write to him. I didn't think they'd passed the letters on, but when he was nine years old, he started to write back. He told me he was in Maple Lakes."

"But you stayed in Ridgemore?"

Sarah sucks in her cheeks and shakes her head, as if the decision to stay weighs heavy on her to this day. "I tried, but I couldn't find work there. Maple Lakes is *not* the kind of town that welcomes un-elementals. Not a single place would employ me. So, I had to stay in Ridgemore."

"No one there knew you were a witch?"

Sarah shakes her head. "No."

"Did you make contact with Nova?"

Again, she shakes her head. "She moved around a lot, and her foster families weren't exactly *welcoming* to outsiders. But I kept an eye on her from a far. Always told myself I'd be there if she needed me."

As Sarah stops talking, I breathe in slowly and try to lace the facts together in my head. Something snags in my brain. "Sarah?"

She meets my eyes.

"Who is Sam's father? This man who got hooked up with H.E.L.?"

For a moment, Sarah doesn't move. Then she glances out to the parking lot, scans it, and checks behind her. "His name is Ragnor Larsen."

Even though I've never heard the name before, something in the way Sarah speaks it makes me shudder. "Is he still with them?"

She nods, almost imperceptibly. "These days, Ragnor *is* the League."

The gravity of what's just happened hits me slowly; for years, we've been searching for a name. For the super who pulls the strings. The super who so desperately wants to end humanity. Just like that, this woman has given it to me.

As Sarah stares into her coffee, more pieces drop into place. I lean closer and duck to meet her eyes. "Sarah... a few days ago, one of my brothers was kidnapped by the League—"

"I don't know anything about that," she says quickly.

"They kidnapped him because they knew Nova would go after him."

She blinks at me slowly.

"They wanted her because they believe she's the key to a prophecy." I pause, scrutinizing Sarah's face for a reaction. "Do you know anything about that prophecy?"

Sarah's muscles stiffen. She looks like she wants to get up and run. Finally, she inhales deeply and says, "Yes. I do."

I wait for her to continue.

"About five years ago, Ragnor came to see me. He was different. I could tell from his eyes. They were darker and there was a blackness around him that made me go cold as soon as I looked at him."

She reaches to start gathering up the pictures, but I stop her; not until she's told me the truth. The whole truth.

"I hadn't been in touch with Sam since his sixteenth birthday. He stopped writing back to me. I spent every cent I had trying to find him. I hired a private detective, then another, then another. But he'd vanished without a trace. Ragnor knew. I don't know how, but he knew." Her face has paled. She looks older all of a sudden. Smaller. "He told me he'd found Sam, and that if I did something for him, he'd tell me where Sam was."

"What did he ask you to do?"

"Watch Nova."

My skin prickles with heat. "*Watch* her?"

Sarah nods. "He remembered what I told him when Alice and Charles were killed. He remembered the voicemail I left... I said that Nova wasn't harmed but that Sam had very bad burns."

"So, when Kole accessed the prophecy for them, that's when Ragnor put the pieces together and decided Nova was the Phoenix."

Sarah frowns at me as if she's got no idea what I'm talking about.

"Phoenix?" she knits her fingers together tightly. "I don't know what the prophecy said. Ragnor never told me. All he told me was that he believed Nova could be *important* to him."

"So, you were to watch her, and then what?"

"I was to watch her, and if anything like the first fire happened again, I was to tell him straight away."

"And then he'd give you Sam?"

Sarah meets my eyes and nods.

"So, when Nova set fire to Johnny's apartment, you got straight on the phone to your friend at the Human Extinction League and told him exactly where she'd gone?"

A sigh ripples through Sarah's shoulders. She hangs her head. "I took her to the bus station. I watched her get on the bus, then I called Ragnor. I told him everything."

"You pretended to be her friend, and you betrayed her."

Sarah looks up at me, her eyes shining with tears. "I didn't know he wanted to hurt her."

I raise my eyebrows.

"I didn't know," she repeats quietly.

"Well, now you do." I take her coffee cup away and shove it toward the window. "So, tell me, where is Sam? Where is Nova's brother?"

Before Sarah can answer me, movement outside in the parking lot catches my eye. A black SUV. No plates. Then another.

I sit up straight, press my back into the leather seat, and watch as it stops at an angle. Sarah has seen it too. She moves as if she's about to get up, but I gesture for her to wait.

I look around. The waitress has disappeared. The entire place is empty. This isn't right... The SUV's doors open. A woman steps out. I recognize her immediately; *Eve.*

Instantly, I'm on my feet, fire in my palm. "We have to go. Now. Out back." I tug Sarah to her feet and head for the bar. Before we reach it, the entire diner begins to shake. Plates fall from shelves, glasses break. Another shock rocks the building. This time, the windows shatter. Sarah cries out and ducks down, covering her head with her hands.

"No time. Move." I jerk her to her feet and drag her into the kitchen. It's empty here too. Someone told the staff to clear out.

We run to the back of the kitchen, but before I can put my hand on the door, it flies off its hinges. Eve is in front of us. She reaches out, twisting her hand as if she's trying to grab hold of my throat from afar. As my breath swells in my chest, and I struggle to breathe, the fire in my hand flickers.

Sarah stands next to me, trembling. Then she takes something from her purse. Long and thin. Is that a friggin' wand?

She points it at Eve, who tilts her head and starts to laugh. But then Sarah whispers something, and Eve is knocked clean off her feet.

I can breathe again. Eve is trying to stand. I hurl a ball of fire into her stomach, and she falls back. Behind us, the sound of wolves trashing the diner makes me grab Sarah's arm and run.

They're all inside now. I run past the SUVs and yell at Sarah to get in as I jump into the car and start the engine. She slides in next to me and pulls the door shut just as Eve stalks around the corner, lightning crackling down her arms, fury in her eyes.

"You can't escape that easily," she shouts.

But she's wrong.

I slam my foot on the pedal and tear out of the parking lot onto the highway. I take the first exit, follow the curve of the road, then tear down a small farm track, through a field, out the other side.

They're not behind us, but I keep driving.

"Do you have anything on you? A cell? A laptop?" I shout.

Sarah blinks at me as if she doesn't understand the question.

"Anything they could have used to track you to the diner?"

Slowly, she lifts her cell phone from her purse. I wind down her window and jerk my head at it. Sarah doesn't hesitate to throw it.

"Anything else?" I ask.

"No," she says. She's clutching her stack of photographs. "Nothing else."

After a moment's silence, I look into the rear-view mirror. "We lost them." I look at her sideways. "It's okay. We lost them."

"They came there to kill me," she says quietly.

"Yes," I say. "They did."

She hugs her waist and sniffs as tears escape her eyes. "I lied to you," she says.

I frown. Did I hear that right?

"I lied about knowing where Sam is."

"But you said—"

"Ragnor never told me. After I called him and told him about Nova, he said he'd call me back. He didn't, and the number he gave me has been disconnected." She laughs to herself and shakes her head. "He used me," she says. "I don't know why I'm surprised. I knew what kind of man he was. I just so badly wanted Sam back in my life." She looks at me pleadingly, willing me to understand.

"So, you didn't call me because you wanted to help Nova? You called because you want *me* to find Sam?"

Sarah closes her eyes and exhales slowly. "Yes," she says. "Please. Help me."

8

TANNER

Mack strides out to the barrier, shifts into Snow, and gives the reporters one hell of a fucking show. Some of them scream and run back through the woods to their cars. Others just zoom in and wax lyrical to their cameras about how the town's sheriff has been taken in by the evil human-killing witch.

Watching it unfold on the TV is a head spin. We're in the ballroom because it's at the rear of the house, far away from the garden and the woods beyond. This side is hemmed in by a wider section of the river and a seven-foot brick wall, so it's not as appealing to the vultures trying to break the protection shield.

Kole is pacing. The veins in his neck twitch when he looks at Nova. "I can bring the trees down," he says, stopping underneath the disco ball so that incongruous dancing lights freckle his face.

He looks up, frowns, and shifts sideways so his face darkens again.

"I could pull every drop of water from the river and wash their camera equipment into the sewer," I snarl, "but Mack said no."

Over by the pool table, Nico clears his throat.

Nova walks over to him and asks if he's okay.

"Fine," he says, smiling at her. "I'm fine. Just a little spooked by all this." He tilts his head toward the TV screen.

As he speaks, I study his face. Since he got here, I've been trying to open the gates in my head. I've searched his emotions, his aura, looking for untruths and concealment because I do *not* trust this guy. Looking for anything I can show Nova to prove she needs to ask a few more questions before falling headfirst into the belief that he's some kind of missing piece in her family puzzle.

For the hundredth time, I come up blank. Wolves are notoriously hard to read, but Nico is different. He's *impossible* to read.

Nova rubs his upper arm and smiles at him. "I'm kinda spooked too. I mean, pretty much every person out there wants to burn me at the stake, right?" She laughs a little, looking from me to Kole.

In a guttural growl, Kole tells her, "Don't say that."

I meet his gaze. She's not wrong; she's being glib, but she's not wrong. They might not be able to tie her to a pole and set fire to her, but the Bureau will be expected to dole out an appropriate punishment. What the masses deem appropriate remains to be seen.

Looking down at her hands, Nova conjures a flame. She's doing it more often lately; practicing. This time, she passes it from one palm to the other. Pulls and plays with it like it's putty.

Nico watches it. When she looks at him, she extinguishes the fire and says, "Does it remind you?"

He tilts his head.

"I mean, do you remember it? The fire?"

Nico shakes his head. "No. I don't remember."

"But you were hurt." She gestures to his chest. "Badly."

Nico smiles softly at her. "I don't remember any pain, Nova. You mustn't think about it."

"Shit," Kole says, pointing at the screen. "Snow's losing it."

On the TV, Snow has just finished mauling a tree and is bellowing at the crowd of reporters. Finally, he stops and stalks back toward the house. The front door opens and closes. Footsteps cross the entrance hall. In moments, Mack is with us. Naked but holding a bundle of clothes he's taken from the hall closet.

Standing behind the pool table, he dresses. His skin is glistening with sweat and his muscles are twitching. "Nova." He grabs her and cups her face in his hands. "We need to go now. Tom's not going to call. It's been too long."

"Asking him to speak to Annalise was a long shot," Kole adds. Looking at Nova, he says, "She was our boss when we were with the Bureau. These days, she's as high up as you can get at the SDB and probably wouldn't even speak to Tom on the phone."

As Mack sighs, Nova leans into his hand. "I'm sorry," she whispers. When she looks up at him, she says, "I could go alone... or with Tanner and Kole." She gestures to the ballroom walls. "This is your home. I don't want to make you leave it."

Mack smiles a little, possibly remembering the last time camera crews were parked up outside. It was years ago, before I got here, but Mack showed me the footage. Maybe someday he'll show Nova. But not now.

"I have a complicated history with this place," he says. "So, trust me, leaving it is not a problem. Especially for you."

"It's not forever." Kole puts his hand on Nova's shoulder, catching Mack's eyes above her head. "Just for now."

"Um, guys..." Nico says. He's pointing at the TV screen. "They've stopped."

In unison, we all turn around. He's right; the line of SUVs has pulled over to the side of the road, and the chopper has disappeared.

We're still staring when Mack's cell goes off. He puts it on speaker. A voice I don't recognize fills the room. "I spoke with Annalise. She vouched for you. I'll come to Phoenix Falls alone.

After sunset. In the meantime, I'll have local officers clear out the reporters."

"Tom…thank you."

"Don't thank me yet, Sheriff. You have a lot of explaining to do. And if I'm not satisfied, we *will* take the girl into custody."

"You did it." Nova turns to Mack and throws her arms around his neck. "You did it!"

"I'm not sure what I did," Mack says, still looking at the TV. "But at the very least, it seems I bought us some time."

"We should still leave." I mute the TV and look at Kole for his agreement. "Right? He just said that if he's not satisfied, he'll take Nova. So, we get her out of here. Mack, you and Luther can talk to Tom alone. Right?"

Mack is rubbing his beard, lost in thought. "I don't know…"

"You don't know?" My temples are throbbing. Since the jump, I've been on the verge of a migraine. I can feel it lingering in the darkness of my mind. The room shifts and splinters momentarily into a kaleidoscope of images. Then it shifts back. I shake my head. "You can't possibly think it's a good idea for her to stay here!"

"If Nova's here, she can tell her side of the story. Plus, it'll be a show of good faith."

"Good faith?" Kole snarls.

"Do you think that'll work?" Nico ventures into the conversation. "I mean, they're SDB agents. Aren't they more concerned with proof? Facts? Irrefutable evidence? Surely, Nova's side of the story isn't going to sway them very far from their current position."

Nico's tone of voice makes me want to strangle him. It's the same tone he uses in his celebrity speeches and at his fancy galas and charity events; patronizing and sycophantic.

"Nico's right," Mack says, pacing over to the window. "We need more than words to convince them. We need—"

"The blood tests." Kole cuts in. He crosses the room in two strides and grabs my arm. "The tests you took Nova for. Did you ever get the results?"

I shake my head. Why the fuck didn't I think of it sooner? For the second time, the room splinters then returns to normal. I reach into my pocket and take a migraine pill. Kole notices but says nothing. "The results, Tanner. Did you get them?"

"No," I say. "But that could be it." I turn to Mack. "If the tests show Nova's got human DNA—"

"Make the call." Mack nods.

Ingrid's cell rings to voicemail six times before she finally answers. She's speaking in a hushed voice. The background is noisy. She's mid-shift. "Tanner? You shouldn't be calling me." She pauses. There's the sound of a door clicking shut and the background noise dims. "I've seen the news. That girl you brought in here, she's the country's most wanted witch right now."

"I know. That's why I need the test results, Ingrid. Have you got them?"

She hesitates, then says, "Yes. I have them, but—"

"Can you send them to me?"

"Tanner..."

"What do they show?"

"Tanner... I'm sorry. I can't get involved. I have to go."

"Ingrid. No. Wait." I raise my voice. "Ingrid—"

"I have a family. If the Bureau found out I was involved... I can't. I'm sorry."

Before I can say anything else, she's gone. When I look at the others, they're staring at me. "She won't help. She's too scared." I flex my fingers at my sides. "It's okay. I'll go."

"Absolutely not." Nova grabs my elbow. "Tanner, the entire town knows you're in here with me. If they do arrest me, won't that make all of you *accessories* or something?" She looks at Mack. His mouth twitches and he nods.

"She's right, Tanner," Mack confirms solemnly.

"And it's not just agents or cops. There are a lot of angry people out there." Nova slides her hand down my arm and slots her fingers between mine. "They could hurt you."

"I can look after myself, Little Star." I press my forehead to hers. "We need this. If the tests show you have human DNA, the Bureau will *have* to back off. They'll have to take the prophecy seriously."

"And if the tests show I'm a witch?" She meets my eyes and searches them for a sign I understand what she's saying. "Then they'll have irrefutable evidence that I broke the treaty. If you're caught and they get hold of that information, it'll make things worse." She shakes her head. "We should stick to Mack's plan— hope my story will be enough." She runs her hand over her chest. She's wearing a tank top and a thick gray cardigan. Her tattoo camouflages the scar beneath it, but we all know it's there. "I have plenty of scars I can show them to prove what Johnny was like."

"I'll go," Nico's voice is small and quiet, almost as if he's talking to himself. As we all turn to look at him, leaning on the sideboard near the TV, he repeats, louder, "I'll go."

He stands up and looks at the TV. His lips break into a smile, and he straightens his shoulders; they look small inside my clothes. "I'm Nico Varlac," he says, the way he might if he was introducing himself on one of those reality TV shows he likes to frequent. "No one will think it's strange that I'm here—in fact, they'd *expect* me to be here."

"That's true," Kole says, looking at the silenced TV screen. "Under any other circumstances, Nico would be out there with the reporters trying to calm the situation down." Pointedly, he says, "That's what he does. Right? Keeps the peace between supers and humans. Smooths the choppy waters when things get rough."

Nico's smile wavers, but he nods. "Exactly."

"Absolutely not." I shake my head, wondering if Mack and Kole have lost theirs for even *considering* letting this guy get involved.

Before Mack can answer me, Nova steps in and says, "Tanner, what do we have to lose?" She softens her voice and inches closer to me.

I narrow my eyes, trying to figure out if she genuinely trusts him enough to let him do this. "If Nico passes the information in those tests to the press or the Bureau—"

Nova closes her eyes, frustration creasing her features. She breathes out slowly. "First of all, why would he do that? He's my brother. Second, even if you're right and he can't be trusted…" She looks to Mack for his agreement. "I still think it's worth the risk." When she turns back, she runs her hand up my chest then strokes my neck. "At least *you* won't be in danger this way."

As Nova and I stare at each other, Nico edges forward. He puts his hand on my shoulder. "Let me do this, Tanner," he says. "Let me prove to you all that you can trust me."

9

NICO

As soon as it's agreed, Tanner reluctantly disappears to fetch his hospital entry card so I can get access to the building. I wait for Mack and Kole to leave, too, to give Nova and me a moment alone, but they don't.

"You're sure about this?" she asks, wrapping her arms around her waist in a movement that makes her breasts swell beneath the rim of her tank top.

I pull my eyes up to her face and nod. "One hundred percent."

"If anyone sees you—"

"I'll do a speech to the camera and tell them I'm here in case I can be useful as a negotiator or intermediary between the witch," I tweak my thumb under her chin, "and the SDB."

Nova nods slowly. "Alright," she says. "But you'll be careful."

"I'll be careful."

When Tanner returns, he hands me the entry card and tells me his login details for the hospital's computer system. "The tablets in the E.R. will be the easiest to get hold of. Swipe one from the desk as you walk past—you'll need my entry card to unlock one. On the left, just before you get to the corridor, are the male washrooms. Go in and lock yourself in a stall." He taps the piece of paper he's given me. "Log in with these. The screen will automatically open to our central database. Every-thing is integrated, so each patient has their own file with access to scans, tests, and notes. You're looking for *Julia Roberts*."

"Julia Roberts?" I look from Tanner to Nova. "Are you serious?"

"Inside joke," Nova says, exchanging a half-smile with Tanner.

"Date of birth, January 1st, 1990."

"It's not my real birthday," Nova says.

"I know." I smile at her, even though I have no clue when her birthday is.

"All set?" Mack asks. In the corner of the room, Kole says noth-ing. Just stares at me.

"All set." I clutch the entry card tight between my fingers. "I just need a little help to get out of here. I'm guessing we can't take the shield down?"

Taking my arm, Mack walks me to the window and points at the wall beyond the section of river that weaves closest to the house.

"How good are werewolves at jumping?" he asks, raising his eyebrow at me.

I tilt my head from side to side. I've never been particularly athletic, never had cause to be, but in wolf form I'm pretty sure I can make it.

"Cross the river. Climb the wall. When you're over, we'll create an opening on that side of the property just long enough for you to get through. Same on the way back. You reach the barrier, you call, we let you back in."

Mack steps in front of me. He thrusts a spare cell phone into my hand. His eyes flash amber. "If you see anyone—*anyone*—who might try to break through while that part of the shield is down, you wait. Got it?"

I nod, moistening my lips. Espionage isn't really my thing. But something deep in my gut tells me this is my chance—a chance to prove to my mother and father that I am worthy.

Everyone here has risked their life more than once, Nico…

Ragnor's voice rings in my ears.

He would want me to do it. He would be proud that I took the initiative to suggest it; not only will I be securing a vital piece of information about Nova, but I'll be buying her trust—and a ticket to follow her wherever her guys take her next.

"I'm ready." I slip the entry card into my pocket. "Just need some sneakers."

Tanner jerks his head toward the door. I follow him. Mack,

Nova, and Kole stay put in the ballroom and head for the window so they can watch me scale the wall.

From the hall closet, Tanner takes a pair of white sneakers. They look too big, but I slip them on.

"Mack's number is programmed in," he says.

I shake his hand. He grips my fingers tightly, then stands and watches me leave.

Outside, the distant click and hum of the news cameras has died down. Their scent still lingers in the air, but it's thinning now. Which means the SDB agent must have kept his word and begun clearing them out.

At the river, I put the entry card and the cell phone between my teeth, and shift in one fluid motion. The water is ice-cold but slow-moving, so I cross the river quickly, careful to keep my head up and out of the water.

On the other side, I shake droplets of moisture from my fur, take a running jump, and scramble over the wall. The drop on the other side is more difficult to judge. I fall awkwardly and yelp as my leg twists beneath me.

I shift back, muscles twitching because I'm forcing it to happen more quickly than normal. My clothes are wet. I put the card in my pocket then text Mack: *Ready*.

The invisible barrier in front of me starts to shimmer. A tear appears, undulating at the edges as if it's made of water. I hold my breath, half expecting to be sliced in two when I step through it. But it works; I'm free.

I look back at the house, towering above the wall. I could run. Right now, I could run. Not just from Nova and The Hollow, or the lies I'm weaving, but from my father too. I could leave all this behind me. Start fresh somewhere new.

But what would I do? What use am I if I'm not serving the League?

I draw my shoulders back and clench my jaw.

Without the League, I am nothing. Without the League, I would be nothing. I am the League.

I have no choice.

10

NOVA

Watching Nico shift, I turn to Mack and put my hands on my hips. "How come your clothes are shredded to pieces when you shift, and Nico's sort of *melt* into his skin?"

A smile curves his mouth. "I have no idea."

"Aren't you supposed to know this stuff, Professor?" I ask, wagging my finger at him.

"Probably." He's standing beside me and allows his fingers to brush mine.

On my other side, Kole checks the time. "I'd estimate at least two hours until he returns. Maybe three."

"That long?" I ask, looking at the sky; it's only five hours 'til sunset, which doesn't feel like a lot of time to spare.

Kole takes out his phone and shows me a map. "It's a forty-five-minute walk from here to the hospital. Could be quicker if he stole some mode of transport, but that wouldn't be a good look. He can skirt around town, but if he's seen and has to stop—"

"That'll add time," I say, biting my lower lip. "So, we just sit and wait?"

Kole looks at Mack, who says, "He promised to email the results to me, so we'll know when he's succeeded. Then he'll text when he's on the way back." He puts his hands in his pockets and inhales deeply. "But, yes, until then we wait."

As Mack speaks, Kole watches the door. Tanner hasn't returned yet. "Maybe he's packing a bag," I offer. "I'll go check—"

"No." Kole's voice is firm. He softens it slightly and repeats, "No, it's okay, Little Star. I'll go. I need to pack too. Just in case we end up having to make a quick exit."

Kole's about to head for the door when he stops, turns back to me, and kisses my forehead. "We'll pack your things too." He cups my face with his large, strong fingers. One of them traces a line on my throat. It sends a shudder through me. Kole licks his lips and swallows hard. When he looks at me like this, it's as if he wants to quite literally devour every inch of me. My body responds instantly. A fizzing sensation settles beneath my skin.

Kole presses his mouth softly to mine. Slowly, he runs his tongue along my lower lip. When he stops kissing me, I'm breathless. My heart is beating fast, the now-familiar sensation of helpless longing beating in my veins.

"I'll be back." He looks at Mack, nods, then strides out of the room.

I watch him leave. My legs are wobbly. I sit down hard on the window seat and lean forward onto my knees, scraping my fingers through my hair. I breathe out heavily. Everything inside me is screaming *follow Kole.*

"Are you handling it okay?" Mack asks. He's standing next to me. When I look up, he adds, "The blood bond? They're.... potent. I can imagine it's hard for you to think of anything else."

As he speaks, his tone is measured, but something flashes in his eyes. I sit up, pushing my hair back over my shoulders. "Do I detect a note of jealousy in your voice, Baloo?"

Mack's eyes crinkle as he frowns, but his mouth betrays the fact he's amused. Trying not to laugh, he shakes his head. "It's bad enough when Tanner uses that ridiculous nickname. Don't you start, Little Star."

I tug his pants leg, just a little, by the knee, so he looks down at me. "Do you prefer 'Daddy'?"

His mouth drops open, then he closes it again and shakes his head. "I don't know where that came from, but it's completely inappropriate." There's the hint of a smile on his lips, and color in his cheeks, but he turns away from me and paces over to the pool table.

I watch him for a moment. He's wearing black jeans and a gray hoodie. The jeans make his ass look incredible. Tilting my head, I wonder whether Kole and Tanner ever think about Mack's ass.

Very quickly, that thought blows my mind into a million dirty pieces and I have to stand up because the tingling between my legs is too much.

"Three hours is a long time to wait," I say as Mack returns to the window to look out at the river.

"It is." He folds his arms in front of his chest but doesn't look at me.

"If only there was something we could do to pass the time…" I lace my hands together behind my back, fully aware that the gesture makes my breasts swell.

Mack still doesn't look at me, but his breathing has quickened.

I turn away from him and walk slowly to the pool table. When I reach it, I stop. My heart is racing. I'm hot and cold all over, and I can't work out whether I'm nervous or just so excited I'm almost nauseous.

Without saying anything, I unfasten my jeans. The black ones Mack gave me. I slide them down over my hips, deliberately jutting out my ass in case he turns around.

I have no idea if he's watching. So, I step carefully out of them, then turn around. He's still facing the window but, as disappointment tugs at my chest, I realize I'm wrong; he's staring at my reflection.

Knowing he's watching a slightly blurry version of my movements gives me the confidence boost I need to sit up on the end of the pool table and open my legs.

Leaving them open so the cool air soothes my tingling core, I use the elastic on my wrist to fasten my hair in a loose bundle at the base of my neck. I tilt my head back and run my hands down my throat. When I reach my shoulders, I slip my cardigan off, then pull my tank top over my head.

My bra is a deep turquoise, the same one I wore in Kole's secret room. As the sun catches the ridiculous disco ball above my head, it casts golden freckles on my chest.

I hold my breath as I wonder what to do next. A slow heat is filling me up, soothing away my self-consciousness and replacing it with something else; the same thing I felt when Kole made me stand in front of his mirror. A sense that it's *okay* to do what feels good. To trust my own body.

By the window, Mack is now leaning on the frame, breathing slowly but heavily. I swallow hard then, in my most forceful voice, tell him, "Daddy, I need your help."

Mack's entire body stiffens. His fingernails scratch the wooden frame as he grips it. "Nova…" he says. "Now's not the time..."

Ignoring him, I trace my finger along the hem of my bra cups.

Mack doesn't move.

"Come here," I tell him, a shiver snaking down my spine as I wait to see if he'll obey me. When he finally turns around, I can see the outline of his erection through his pants. "Come here," I tell him again, curling my finger to beckon him over.

He walks to me as if he's still trying to resist but doesn't know how to. He stops and drinks in my almost-naked body. "Fuck," he breathes, swiping his fingers through his salt and pepper hair. "This isn't fair, Nova."

"No," I say, "it's not." I shift back a little, opening my legs wider. "I really do need your help."

A noise like a growl escapes Mack's lips.

"I need you to take care of me, Daddy."

He wavers for a moment, then strides forward as if he's going to grab me. He stops with his hands quivering above my arms. Lowering them to his sides, he meets my eyes and says, "Tell me what you need."

My core pulses with arousal as I realize he won't give in, but he *will* do what I ask. I look down at my bra. "Take this off."

Mack slides his hands around me and, with one flick, unfastens it. His thumbs linger on my skin as he tucks his fingers beneath the straps and helps the bra to fall. Instead of tossing it to the ground, he places it gently beside me. Taking his cell from his pocket, he puts it purposefully on top, letting me know he's not off duty; the second Nico contacts him, he'll be ready.

Then he straightens his shoulders and meets my eyes. He's standing in front of me, hands behind his back like a bodyguard or a soldier, waiting for me to tell him what to do next. I close my eyes and lean back onto my hands, so my chest moves up toward him. "Put your mouth on me," I sigh.

Mack doesn't hesitate. He dips his head and, as if suddenly he's the student and I'm grading him on his performance, licks a deliberate line up between my breasts. The warmth of his tongue makes my skin flicker in response. Looking up at me, meeting my eyes, he swirls his tongue around my nipple but purposefully doesn't close his mouth over it. The sight of him teasing me forces a groan from my lips.

Firmly, Mack cups my breast with both hands, then closes his eyes. He breathes out hard as I weave my fingers into his hair and pull him to me. Finally, he starts to suck. His tongue works in circles that send shivers of electricity down through my body. When the heat of his mouth disappears, I moan, but then it's back, lapping both breasts at the same time as he pushes them together.

Without speaking, I tug at his hoodie and he pulls it off and tosses it to the floor. His shoulders ripple as he returns to my body, kissing my stomach softly, carefully.

In my whole life, I don't think anyone has ever kissed my stomach before; it's the part I usually cover up. But Mack is determined to kiss every inch.

When he reaches my hips, before he can remove my underwear, I sit up and smooth my hands over his torso, admiring the groove of his muscles. "My turn," I tell him.

He drops his hands to his sides and watches as I return the gesture, swirling my tongue over his chest. He sighs loudly when I gently bite his nipple, then he clenches his fists. "Nova…"

His chest is peppered with hair. Not as thick as Kole's, but thicker than Tanner's. I press a fingernail to his skin and trace a line from his chest to his belly button. When I increase the pressure, sparks flutter between us.

Through his pants, I cup his balls and apply just the smallest amount of pressure.

"By the moon, Nova…" He nudges my chin with his thumb, stares into my eyes, then says, "May I kiss you?"

I nod. "Yes, please, Daddy."

For a moment, Mack closes his eyes as if the force of my words takes him to the edge of losing control. He's hesitant as he brushes his lips against mine, but then he tugs my hair and wraps his arms tight around me. I reach for the waist of his jeans, but he stops my hands. "Lie back," he whispers, his lips now close to my ear. "Let me make you spark."

I do as he says, stretching my arms up over my head while I press my back to the table. Mack's hands are on my waist. They move to my hips. He nudges me to the edge of the table, then bends my knees and pushes my underwear to one side.

"Is this for me?" he asks, trailing a gentle finger down my cunt, through the wetness. "Or was it Kole? When he kissed you?"

I can barely speak. I scrape my fingers against the surface of the table. "Both of you," I say. "It's for both of you."

Mack pauses. When I look up, he leans over me, his broad shoulders and thick arms forming an arch above my chest. He parts my lips with his, then slides his finger into my mouth.

"Can you taste yourself?" he asks, watching my face.

I suck on his finger and nod. When he takes it away, I tilt my hips and push them against his. I reach for his waist. I want him inside me. But he shakes his head and moves back down my body. Bending over, he lowers his mouth to nibble my inner thighs.

He teases me for a long time. Too long.

When he finally eases a finger inside me, I have no idea who's in control anymore. A moment ago, it was me. But now I can't tell if I'm the one surrendering or if it's Mack.

All I know is that I never want it to stop.

11

KOLE

"Tell me the truth." I'm towering over Tanner, who's sitting on the edge of the bed. "Are you alright?" My voice is harsh, gruff, and not as caring as it should be. I try to soften it. "Tanner, I need to know if you're alright."

When he looks up, he nods. "I'm okay. Just recalibrating."

I sit down next to him and put my hand on his thigh. "I know what you did for me and Nova… to find us." I tilt my head as a chuckle ripples through my chest. "Well, okay, it was probably all for Nova but… you jumped, right?"

Tanner nods then says, "It was for both of you," nudging me with his shoulder. "I did it for both of you."

I squeeze his leg. "I'm sorry you had to revisit that place. Thank you."

Tanner gets up and starts removing clothes from the dresser, loading them into a black duffel. Last time he went to the cabin, it was with the intention of it being a short trip. This time, we're both aware it could be more long-term if Mack can't pull the Bureau over to our side.

"I jumped twice." Tanner's back is facing me. His voice is quiet.

"Twice?" I stand up and move so he is forced to look at me. "How's that even possible?"

Tanner shrugs, but his face is pale. "I'm okay," he says, a little shakily. "I'm okay. I just need these headaches to shift so I can focus on Nico. I can't get a reading from him. I keep trying but—"

"Wolves are always hard to read," I tell him. "Don't overdo it." I look down at him, studying his face. It's different. His eyes are nervous, unfocused. "I know what it's like to fight a demon inside," I say quietly, pressing my palm to his chest. "I can help."

"I'm okay." Tanner closes his eyes. His hand moves to my waist. He leans into me. His mouth is on my neck when I hear Nova.

A scream. Downstairs.

We lock eyes and run from the room. It came from the back of the house. The ballroom.

"Nova?!" Tanner calls. But when we reach the door, he stops. He turns around and puts his hands on my arms to stop me from barging through it.

"What?" My veins are throbbing. I want to rip the door off its hinges. "What is it?"

But Tanner's not worried anymore; he's smiling. "She's not hurt," he says quietly, closing his eyes so I know he's letting her feelings wash over him. "She's with Mack."

I raise my eyebrows.

Tanner grips the handle.

I'm about to stop him when I hear her again. This time, she's not yelling, she's pleading. "Daddy, don't stop…"

I look at Tanner. He adjusts his cock in his pants and laughs as he lightly thumps the wall. "Hearing her call the professor 'Daddy' should *not* turn me on but—"

I know you're there. Nova's voice in my head drowns out Tanner's. *Are you going to come in?*

12

NOVA

Mack's tongue has brought stars to my eyes. As he expertly sucks and nibbles my clit, he hooks his fingers inside me, and the movement makes me yelp with pleasure. "Daddy, don't stop," I shout too loud, but who the hell cares?

Then something else rushes through me. A force that freezes my breath in my lungs and makes my entire body tense.

Mack feels me stiffen beneath him and stops. He runs his hands up my body and cups my face. "Nova? Did I hurt you?"

I shake my head. I can't speak. Mack's erection is pressing into me now, but it's still trapped inside his pants; every time I try to remove them, he stops me.

"We have company," I tell him, holding on tight, running my hands down his back, taking the moment to catch my breath.

As the door opens, Mack stands, offering me his hand so I can sit up. I wrap my legs around his waist and peer out from behind him. Tanner and Kole are in the doorway. Tanner is grinning. Kole isn't, but he's not pissed; he's drinking us in.

Mack hasn't looked at the boys but moves to pull away from me.

I tighten my grip on his waist, clenching him with my thighs. I take his hand and slide it back between my legs. "You brought me so close. You can't leave now."

Mack sighs as he presses his forehead to mine. Then, hands appear on his waist. Tanner's hands. Mack doesn't take his eyes from me. I expect him to be surprised by Tanner's touch, but he leans into it.

Tanner tugs Mack's pants, and his impressive length finally springs free. Instantly, my hands go to his shaft. I hop down and kneel in front of him, running my fingers up the inside of his legs until I reach his balls. He turns and leans back against the pool table, tilting his hips for me.

Gently massaging Mack's balls, I lower my tongue to his slick red tip. I close my mouth over him and take as much as I can before he hits the back of my throat.

I open my eyes to see Tanner beside me. He strokes my hair from my face, kissing my forehead with a grin, then holds my mouth open so Mack can plunge in and out of it.

The sensation of Tanner's tender hands holding me, while Mack finally loses control and fucks my mouth, makes me reach for my pussy.

Don't. Kole's voice vibrates in my head. *Your cunt is for us.*

I search for him. I can't see him, but then I feel his hands. He's pulling me up onto all fours. His fingers find my clit and begins to play with it, but I don't want that. I want to feel full. I need to feel full.

"She wants you to fuck her," Tanner says, looking at Kole over my head before meeting my wide-eyed gaze. "Isn't that right, Little Star?"

I nod, taking Mack's wet cock out of my mouth and angling my head so I can soothe his balls with my tongue.

Gently, Kole runs a finger down between my ass cheeks. For a moment I tense, thinking he's going to ease into my tight, previously un-fucked, hole; the hole I promised to Tanner. But he doesn't. He kneels on one leg, so he's towering above me, then slams into my pussy so hard I jolt forward.

Tanner catches me. His hands move from my arms to my tits. As they sway with the rhythm of Kole's dick, he brushes his thumbs over my sensitive pink buds. Then he kisses me. Deep and hard.

I moan into Tanner's mouth, then break away from the kiss to see Mack fisting his dick, watching as Kole slides in and out of me, one hand on my ass and the other on my shoulder so he can pull me onto him again and again.

Tanner stands and pulls off his clothes. Seeing him and Mack completely naked, next to one another, I feel like reaching for my phone and taking a picture so I can remember this moment forever and ever. Never in my life did I think I'd find *one* guy this hot. Let alone three. Mack's silvery hair and neat beard next to Tanner's smoothness are like two sides of a coin. They complete a whole I didn't know I needed until this exact moment.

In unison, they move closer. Their shafts touch as they hold them in front of me. Their tips glistening with pre-cum. Balanced by Kole's strong hands, I slide my own up the outside of their dicks, pushing them together. Then I swipe my tongue over their slits. Mack tightens his grip and starts to move his knuckles up and down. Gently, Tanner nudges the side of my face with his cock. When I smile, he slaps a little harder.

This makes Mack groan and put his hand on my head, easing himself back into my mouth while Tanner teases my cheeks and my chin with his erection.

As Kole tilts his hips, he reaches around and puts pressure on my clit with the palm of his hand. I squeal and jolt back onto him. He grabs my arms and pulls me so I'm kneeling upright with my back pressed against his chest. Mack and Tanner sink to the floor and bring their mouths to my nipples.

Kole stops touching me. His warmth leaves my clit, but then Tanner's fingers are there instead and, when I look down, Kole's hand is wrapped around Tanner's thick length.

Next to Tanner, Mack starts to pant. Hard. He's going to come.

He stands up, moves to turn away, but I grab his free hand. The other is around his shaft, moving faster and harder as he looks down at me.

Smiling at him, I say, "Come for me, Daddy."

And that's it. He yells a deep, throaty—almost pained—yelp as thick white cum covers my chest.

While Mack staggers backward, I brace my hands on Tanner's shoulders and steady myself as I grind back onto Kole's pulsing dick. He's ready to come too. I can feel it. He wraps his arms around my waist, tightening his grip on me as if it will help him hold down the orgasm building in his core.

When Tanner stands and moves sideways, bringing Kole's mouth to his dick as I play with his balls, they both release growls that rattle the disco ball above our heads.

Tanner comes in Kole's mouth. At the same moment, my body collapses and an orgasm rips through me. Everything convulses. My inside walls spasm around Kole's dick and pulses of lightning shoot up my spine. He pulls me down onto him. Then something sharp pinches the groove between my shoulder and my neck. At first, it makes me wince. But the pain changes to something else.

"Kole..." I hear Tanner's voice, but it's distant.

I reach back and feel Kole's head nuzzling into me. I hold him down. His mouth on my neck.

"Kole…" Mack is shouting now too. I know he's shouting and yet his voice is quiet.

Will you give yourself to me, Little Star? Kole's words wrap themselves around my limbs.

Always, I tell him.

Heat floods through me. My fading orgasm returns, sweeping back up my body. I cry out and ride this orgasm like a wave before I go limp in Kole's arms. His hands roam my skin. Pulling me close, washing over me, covering every inch. Pain turns to pleasure and back into pain.

Then he's gone. I drop onto all fours, panting hard. Something hot drips down my neck onto the floor. As my eyes focus, I stare at it. Small red droplets.

Blood.

13

LUTHER

In the passenger seat, Sarah looks ready to throw up. "What are you going to do?" she asks quietly.

"I haven't decided yet." I tighten my grip on the steering wheel. "But I can't take you back to The Hollow. Nico's there and I don't want you at more risk than you already are."

Sarah nods gratefully but seems surprised that I care whether she's at risk or not.

"I'll take you someplace safe. I have the recording of what you told me in the diner." I pull onto the road that leads to the back of the stores on Main Street and slow down. When I stop at the rear of *Rev's Threads*, I take out my phone. "I won't take your photos, but can I take pictures of them?"

Sarah nods and reaches into her purse. She's still shaky. Her hands tremble as she passes me the images.

One by one, I snap shots to show Nova. Then I hold up the phone. "If you want to give Nova a message, I'll record it."

For a moment, Sarah doesn't move. Then she nods her head. I press record and she says, "Please believe me when I say I'm sorry. I hope I get the chance to make this up to you."

"That's it?" I ask, stopping the video.

She nods.

"Okay, then let's get you inside." As I open the door and climb out onto the sidewalk, Rev appears at the store's back entrance.

"When you said you had a witness for me to hide, I was expecting someone a little more dangerous-looking," she says, her forehead creasing as she looks at Sarah.

"It's a long story." I turn to Sarah as she steps up onto the sidewalk. "This is Rev. She'll take care of you until I've spoken to Nova and figured out what happens next."

She presses her lips together. She's holding her cardigan tight around her middle. "Alright." She hesitates then, unable to stop herself, says, "And Sam?"

I narrow my eyes. "I don't know." To Rev, I add, "I'll update you when I've spoken with the others."

Rev nods, then watches me get in the car. As I drive away, she's putting her arm around Sarah's shoulders and ushering her inside.

The road out of town is thick with parked-up news crews. They line the sides of the road, reporters on cell phones shouting angrily at fuck-knows-who. Further up, I reach the reason they're all so pissed; a blockade.

I wind down my window to find Daryl's pock-marked face staring back at me. "Deputy Ross?" His pale mouth drops open. "Shoot. Sir, what are you doing out here?" He looks back in The Hollow's direction, which sits just out of sight around the bend. "You're supposed to be in there with the sheriff."

"I am?" I raise my eyebrows at him.

"Well, I mean, I thought…" Daryl trails off.

"What's going on here, Daryl?" I ask sternly, glad I trusted my instincts and dropped Sarah at Rev's.

"The SDB ordered all reporters and news crews to be moved back from the barrier, Sir."

"The SDB?" I drum my fingers on the steering wheel. Mack must have got through to them. At fucking last.

"Yes, Sir."

"Great. In that case, I'll head home. If that's okay with you?" I wait for Daryl's answer.

Daryl holds up a finger. "Wait a minute," he says. "I better check." As I rub my hand over my face and groan with impatience, Daryl gesticulates wildly to Tanya and Jake. They're mid-shouting-match with an angry looking female journalist from Wolf News. Tanya looks past Daryl, sees me, and waves her hand at him.

When he returns to the car, he says croakily, "Tanya says to go ahead and let you past, Sir."

"Very good." I'm about to put the window back up when he says, "For the record, Sir, I don't believe a word of what they're saying about you and the sheriff." He grins a toothy grin and waves his hands. "Team Sheriff. All the way."

I ignore him and press my foot to the gas.

When I reach the driveway, I park just outside the gates. Instead of going up the driveway, I loop around on foot and head for the woods. When I reach the barrier, I press my palms to it, close my eyes, and whisper the incantation key. As soon as I'm through, the portal seals again.

The state of the trees tells me Snow's been having fun terrorizing the news crews. Probably not the best idea, but better than full-on attacking them.

I sprint up to the house. The rush of adrenaline makes me feel alive. Before Nova came to town, I ran ten miles a day. Since she arrived, things have been too chaotic for routine exercise.

I stop at the bottom of the steps, near the fountain, looking up at the house. There's something different about it. Heat quivers around it like a mirage in a desert.

Nova.

I take the stairs two at a time and emerge in the kitchen. The warmth calls to me. I follow it, the air growing thicker, fire itching inside my skin, clawing to be released.

When I reach the ballroom, I stop. I put my hand on the door. My palm is so hot it sizzles against the wood. I push it open and stop in the doorway.

Nova is on the floor. Naked. Mack has his arms around her, also naked. In fact, all of them are fucking naked.

I'm about to yell at them to pull themselves together because we've got a fucking emergency here, when I realize Kole is pressed up against the wall. Tanner has his hands on his shoulders. Kole isn't moving, but his eyes are two black pools staring at Nova.

Mack sees me and helps Nova to her feet. She looks spaced out; doesn't seem to care that her entire body is on display.

My cock pays attention as Mack brings to her to me. A rush of heat floods my balls. She's perfect. Every inch. Then I notice the blood trickling down her neck and merging with the ink on her chest.

"Shit."

Mack meets my eyes. "Take her." He leaves her for a moment,

grabs a blanket from the window seat, then wraps it around her shoulders. As it shields her breasts from view, I swallow hard.

"What the fuck happened?" I bark.

"I'll explain." Mack looks sheepishly down at his semi-hard dick. "Just give us a minute."

Nova follows me quietly down the hall. One we're upstairs, in Mack's room—because it's the biggest—I sit her down on the bed and fetch a cloth from the bathroom.

"Here." I offer it to her. She doesn't seem to hear me.

Kneeling in front of her, I try not to think about the fact I'm between her legs, and press the cloth to her neck. A bite mark. Not the kind a vamp would leave; theirs are like two small puncture wounds. This one is messier. A bruise is already forming around it.

"Wait there." I go back to the bathroom, dampen the cloth, then return and try to mop the drying blood from her skin. I follow the line down her neck to her chest. When I smooth the cloth over her tattoo, she blinks and it's like she's come back to life.

"Luther?"

She looks down at my hand, close to her naked chest. She sees the blood-red stain on the cloth, then gently touches her fingers to her neck. "Kole," she whispers.

"What happened?" I ask, letting her take the cloth as I stand up and fold my arms in front of my chest.

She looks over at the door. "Where are the others?"

"Figuring out whether Kole needs to be chained in the basement again, if I had to guess." Fury laps at my insides. The world is falling apart; the entire town thinks she's a human-killer, and she's spending her time getting down and dirty with my house-mates? And what were *they* thinking?!

Nova doesn't say anything, just pulls the blanket closer and stares at the door. A moment later, as if she knew, Mack and the others enter.

They're now fully dressed, each with a mixture of raw satisfaction and guilt on their faces.

"Kole?" Nova stands and steps toward him, then flicks her eyes to Tanner.

He nods at her. "It's okay. He's okay."

"Fuck knows how," Mack adds in a growl. "But he is."

Pulling Nova into his arms, Kole brushes his thumb over her neck. He doesn't speak, just stares into her eyes. She stares back, then folds herself into his embrace.

"Here." Tanner hands her a bundle of clothes, kissing her temple when she takes them from him.

"I'll change." She gestures to the bathroom.

When she's inside with the door locked, I turn to the others and shake my head at them. "Seriously? What the hell were you thinking?" I wave at the window. "The town's swarming with reporters, the SDB is on its way, Nova's all over the news, and you four decide it's a good time to—"

"The SDB isn't coming." Mack interrupts me. "Tom finally listened to me. He called them off. He's coming alone at sunset."

"Alone?"

Mack nods.

"Right." I search their faces. "Okay, so putting aside the SDB and the fact Kole just *bit* Nova and seems to be totally fine, where's our friend Nico? You just left him to his own devices while you had your little party back there?"

"Nico went to the hospital." Nova appears behind me, arms folded. "He volunteered to retrieve my blood test results, so we can prove I'm telling the truth about being human."

My mouth drops open a little. I laugh and rub my hand over my closely shaved head.

"Luther?" Mack asks, "What's going on?"

I breathe in slowly. I don't even know where to start and, after what I just saw, my head is a mess. "When did he leave?"

"About an hour ago," Nova says. "We're waiting for him to email the results to Mack."

"Then we have time to talk." I point to the door. "Downstairs. Kitchen. Coffee. This is going to be a lot to digest. You'll need the caffeine."

14

NOVA

In the kitchen, Mack makes coffee, but no one sits down. Tanner stands next to Kole, watching him carefully. I put my hand on Mack's back and stroke it lightly. He looks at me over his shoulder, his eyes grazing the mark on my neck. He smiles and brushes my hair from my face. "You're okay?" he asks.

"I'm okay." I turn and look at the others. "Really."

I can still taste you. Kole's voice catches my focus and slithers through my body.

"Are you sure you're alright?" I ask him, hoping that if I stick to out-loud questions, I might be able to ignore the tugging sensation in my stomach that takes hold when I look at him.

"I'm alright, Little Star. I'm sorry if I—"

"We don't have time for this." Luther stands in the middle of us all. He's almost as tall as Kole, with bulky upper arms and runner's legs. "Do you need a meeting?" he snaps at Kole.

Kole's throat makes a grumbling sound.

"You just drank from her. The last time you got within a sniffing distance of her blood, you went full-on vamp. And we don't have time for you to lose it. Not now. So, I'm asking... do you need a meeting?"

The air quivers as Kole and Luther stare at one another. "No," Kole says stiffly. "I don't."

"Fine." Luther nods for Mack to hand out the coffee, then turns to me. "You'll want to sit down."

"I'm fine right here," I say defiantly, leaning back against the countertop, pissed that he's walked in here and started giving orders.

Next to me, Mack takes a deep sip from his mug and watches Luther carefully.

"Alright," Luther says. "I got a phone call yesterday from someone you know."

I frown at him; I barely *know* anyone.

"Sarah Borello." His eyes search my face for a flicker of recognition.

"Sarah? My neighbor?"

Luther nods. He's taken his phone from his pocket. "Sarah told me she knew about your brother—Sam. She said she had information about him and wanted to meet me." He looks at Mack. "That's where I was this morning."

Mack puts his coffee cup down and folds his arms, listening intently.

"She told me a lot." Luther shakes his head. "A *lot*." He hands me the phone. "I recorded it. I didn't think you'd believe me if I told you myself."

I take the phone and stare at it. A big red 'play' button stares back at me. The recording is fourteen minutes and thirty-three seconds long.

"I told you—you might want to sit down." Luther gestures to the table.

Without looking at him, I stride past and sit down. Coffee spills over the rim of my mug when I thump it on the tabletop. Tanner, Kole, and Mack come to join me, but Luther remains standing, cradling his coffee. He looks nervous.

I press play.

Sarah's voice, tinny coming from the phone's small speakers, fills my ears.

"Twenty-four years ago, I was working as a midwife. I was on a night shift. It was late; nearly midnight. It was raining. The kind of rain where you can barely see your hand in front of your face..."

As I listen to Sarah telling her story, the rest of the room disappears. It's like I'm sitting in a black hole. I can't hear anything except her voice. I can't *see* anything.

Toward the end of the recording, when Sarah says the name 'Ragnor Larsen', Mack inhales sharply and bangs the table with his fist. Kole mutters, "Holy crap," and Tanner's eyes widen.

"We've been searching for that name for years," Mack says, but Luther shakes his head and tells him to keep listening.

There's barely a minute left when Sarah tells Luther the truth; that she was watching me for Ragnor. The entire time we were neighbors, she was spying, waiting for my powers to show themselves so she could report back to the League in exchange for Sam's location.

"I took her to the bus station. I watched her get on the bus, then I called Ragnor. I told him everything." Sarah's voice trembles.

Luther sounds disgusted. *"You pretended to be her friend, and you betrayed her."*

"I didn't know he wanted to hurt her."

I stand up and pace toward the door, waving my hand for them to stop the recording. "I don't want to hear anymore. I can't…"

Reaching over the others, Luther presses stop. "There isn't much more to hear," he says darkly. "Shortly after that, we were interrupted by Eve and her werewolf pals."

"Eve?" Kole sits up straighter in his chair and laces his fingers together. "She was there?"

"Tracked Sarah to the diner. We escaped, obviously, thanks to Sarah's wand."

"Wand?" Mack asks.

While Luther launches into something I don't understand—telling the others that Sarah is an *un*-elemental witch who must have bought the wand on the black market—Tanner walks over to me. He doesn't hug me or hold my hand, just stands in front of me, close, so I know he's there.

My thoughts are racing.

Sarah, one of the few people from Ridgemore who I believed to be my friend, is a liar. She used me. "I don't understand." I stride over to Luther and fold my arms in front of my stomach. "Sarah said she wanted to tell you about Sam?"

Luther nodded.

"All this time, she's been searching for him?"

Again, Luther nods, watching me as I try to put the pieces together.

"But surely, she's seen the TV? If she was so close to Sam, why didn't she recognize that he's now going by the name of Nico?" I shake my head. "This doesn't make sense."

Luther's jaw twitches impatiently. "Nova, she didn't recognize Nico because he is *not* Sam."

A laugh bubbles up in my chest. "Of course, he's Sam. He has the burns, and the birthmark. And I *know* it's him… nothing Sarah said proves that Nico isn't Sam."

"Except that Sam went missing when he was sixteen and she hasn't heard from him since." Luther inhales slowly like he's trying to bite down a clot of frustration. "Nova, she told me explicitly that Nico is *not* your brother."

"That wasn't on the tape." I square up to him. He's hated Nico from the moment he saw him; they all have. But I *know* Nico's my brother. I feel it. There's a connection between us, something completely different from what I feel for Tanner, or Kole, or Mack.

As rage builds in my gut, smoke plumes on my skin. It swirls into the room. Luther moves closer. He's head and shoulders taller than me. Fire flashes in his eyes. The heat coming off him meets the heat coming off me and the air between us starts to shimmer.

"Guys, calm down." Tanner gently takes hold of my arms, inching me backwards.

Kole crosses the room and smooths his hands over my arms, flinching at the heat that scalds his palms. "It's okay, Little Star, we'll figure it out," he whispers, close to my neck.

"We *really* don't have time for this." Luther swipes his phone open again. He jerks it at me, and I take it. "Sarah had these with her. Pictures of you and Sam, and your parents. It's undeniable that he and Nico share a resemblance. But they're not the same person, Nova… just look."

Reluctantly, I scroll through the images. When I reach one of me, my parents, and Sam, my legs give way and I drop to the floor.

"It's been years since I saw a picture of them," I whisper as Tanner sinks down next to me. My eyes fill quickly with tears. Hot and salty, they stream down my cheeks. "Johnny destroyed the only photo I had." I run my thumb over the screen. "Isn't she beautiful?" I ask, staring at my mother.

"She is." Tanner leans closer. Gently, he pinches the image and zooms in on Sam. "There…" he points to his wrist. "The birthmark." He looks up at Luther. "Nico has the same one, Luther. I don't like the guy, but maybe—"

"Which wrist?" Luther's question is sharp and pointed and hangs in the air. Kole and Mack move closer, too, and peer over my shoulder at the phone.

I swallow hard and close my eyes. "Sam's birthmark is on his left wrist," I whisper.

"And Nico's?" Luther asks, crouching down and fixing his eyes on mine. The fire is gone now. He's softened. So have I. "Which wrist is Nico's birthmark on, Nova?"

I look from Luther to Tanner and wipe the tears from my cheeks. "Nico's birthmark is on his right." I pass the phone back to Luther. "It's on his right."

Betrayal turns quickly to fury. I scream and hurl a swirling ball of fire across the kitchen. Tanner dampens it before it catches anything alight.

"They faked the burns? The birthmark?" I can barely breathe. I'm pacing back and forth. My chest is tight. My lungs constricting. I shake my arms. Flames lap at my veins, desperate to be free.

"Nova, remember what we practiced." Mack sidesteps in front of me but I push him aside and hurtle out the front door. I need cold air on my face. I need to breathe.

When I reach the fountain, I grip the rim of the basin. Steam rises from the water inside it.

"Breathe." Luther is there. He puts his hands on my shoulders. Standing behind me, he says, "Breathe through the fire. Imagine a cold wind sweeping through your body, putting out the flames." He counts to four, inhaling slowly. I copy the movement of his chest against my back.

As the flames subside, so does the tension I've been holding in my shoulders. Deflated, I turn around and lean back against the edge of the fountain. The water is no longer steaming hot. A cool spray dances on my neck.

"Alright?" Luther asks firmly.

I nod, suddenly self-conscious beneath his gaze.

Mack, Kole, and Tanner are watching us from the kitchen. When I look over at them, they trot down the steps and gather around me.

"I'm sorry," I say quietly. "I'm just so… *humiliated.*" I shake my head, a bitter laugh shaking my chest. "I can't believe how easily he fooled me. And I fell for it. The whole fucking thing." I pause then, a little more quietly, add, "I really believed he was my brother. I really believed he was Sam."

"Nova, they played you. They knew what they were doing," Kole says. He was on that stage with me; he alone knows what it was like up there. "They timed it exactly right. You were primed, your emotions running close to the surface. They wanted a reaction from you, and they used Nico to get it."

I slot my hand into Tanner's and squeeze. He sits down next to me and puts his arm around my waist, diverting the water with a flick of his hand so its spray doesn't dampen my clothes.

"I brought him right back here to live in our midst." My mouth is suddenly dry. "And now he's at the hospital, accessing my files…" I look at Tanner. "Can we stop him? Can you call them?"

He scrapes his fingers through his hair. "I can try—"

But before he can finish, Mack's cell pings him a notification. The delicate sound seems loud out here in the open. Mack takes his phone from his pocket and looks at it. "It says, '*Can't email tests. On my way back. Will call when I'm at the barrier. Nico.*'"

As he reads it, Luther's face darkens.

"You think it's a ploy to stop us from realizing that he's running straight back to the League with my blood test results?" I ask Mack.

Mack strokes his neat gray beard and exhales heavily. "Maybe, or maybe he really will come back here and try to maintain his cover."

Cutting in, Kole says, "He said he wanted to prove we could trust him. So, maybe that's exactly what he's planning."

"He knows we don't trust him," Tanner agrees, miraculously without any hint of 'I told you so' in his voice. "If he brings the tests back, he knows he'll cement his place in the group."

I shudder as a droplet of water from the fountain hits my neck and trickles down beneath my clothes. "So," I say, looking at each of the guys, "what do we do now?"

15

LUTHER

While Mack and the others head inside to finish packing their bags to be ready for a quick exit if things don't go the way Mack hopes with Tom Haze, I stay in the kitchen with Nova.

She still has hold of my phone. She's been staring at the photograph of her parents. I sit down opposite her. "I'll send it to you."

"Thank you," she says, without looking up.

Interrupting her gaze, I reach for the phone. She frowns, but I dip my head to meet her eyes and say, "There's a video message from Sarah if you'd like to see it."

Nova hesitates. She shivers. I get up and close the doors; Mack has a thing about leaving them open, but the summer nights are drawing in and I've always preferred heat to chills.

She hasn't said yes to viewing the video, but I show it to her anyway. She tilts her head as she watches, then wrinkles her nose. "You filmed this in your car?"

I nod.

"Where is she now? Where did you take her?"

"She's in town with Rev."

Nova raises her eyebrows.

"I wanted her close by but didn't think it was a good idea to bring her here. She's already in danger. My guess is that now that Ragnor is finished with her, he wants her out of the way so she can't spill his secrets."

"Bit late for that," she says.

I gesture to her coffee. "Do you want that?"

She shakes her head. "I'll make another. It's cold."

Gently, I touch my finger to the outside of the mug. The liquid heats almost instantly. "Not anymore," I say softly as I push it toward her.

"Thanks." She smiles and adds two large spoonsful of sugar. As she drinks, her top lip hugs the rim of the cup.

For a moment, we sit in silence. She glances at the clock. Any minute now, if he really does intend to come back, Nico will return. "Luther?" Nova says quietly. "Sarah said Ragnor promised to tell her where Sam disappeared to…"

I've been waiting for this question.

"Did he keep his promise?"

"No. He didn't." I don't choose my words carefully; at this stage, I'm pretty sure all Nova wants is the truth. "He disconnected his number."

"But she said she knew where he was?"

"She lied. Again." I lean back in my chair, resting my hands on the table. "I do believe she wanted you to know the truth, Nova. But I also believe she called me because she's out of options."

"She thought you could help find him?"

I nod. "Yes."

"Can you? Find him?"

I take the phone back and stuff it into my pocket. "Sarah hired a private detective. *Several* detectives. She spent every last dime trying to track Sam down. So, wherever he is, it's not going to be easy."

"Will you try? You and Mack?" Nova pulls her hair over her shoulder and smooths it between her hands. "I know we have bigger things to deal with right now, but... he's all I have left of my family. If he's out there, and if he's in trouble, I need to know."

Since the moment she walked into town, I've refrained from looking into this human's eyes for too long. But now, I look.

Really look. They flicker with the same heat I've seen in my own.

"I'll talk to Mack," I tell her. "But we've got some hurdles to jump first."

"Nico," she breathes.

"And the Bureau."

She looks out at the fountain. It won't be long before sunset. "If he's been lying, why hasn't Tanner felt it? I know he doesn't like him, but wouldn't he have known if Nico was..." She sighs, shaking her head.

"He lied, Nova. Tanner didn't feel it because Nico hid it from him."

"I didn't know that was possible."

"It takes practice. Wolves are hard to read at the best of times, and they're good at masking."

"Right." She smooths her thumbs over the sides of her mug. As she opens her mouth to say something else, Mack appears with his phone in his hand.

"He just texted. He's at the wall."

I raise my eyebrows. "He came back?" I didn't expect that.

Mack nods. "Seems like it."

A moment later, Kole and Tanner appear behind him. Kole moves straight to the table and puts his large hands on Nova's shoulders. His finger brushes the bruise on her neck.

"Did he email you the results?" I ask Mack, trying not to think about what the hell happens now that Kole has tasted Nova's blood.

"No. He said it wouldn't work. Said he'd printed them."

"Okay," I reply quietly. "So, no one does *anything* to let him know we're suspicious until we have that printout."

"Get him inside. Get the test results. Then we'll restrain him," Mack offers.

"Mack, our restraining privileges have been removed," I remind him. "If we use police spells, we'll—"

"Be suspended?" Mack laughs ironically and rolls his eyes.

I nod, biting my lower lip. Fair enough. We're already in a shit load of trouble. Might as well throw all caution out of the window.

We settle into silence and watch the lawn. After a few minutes, Nico appears. He shifts by the fountain and strides up to the house dripping wet from the river.

He takes the steps two at a time. When he reaches the top, he waves. He's smiling. The asshole is smiling. So, we smile too.

"Hey, what a welcome party." Nico pushes the doors open and grins broadly at us. "Luther, welcome back, man. You okay?"

I raise my eyebrows at him. "Good. You? I heard you were assigned an undercover mission?"

Nico's eyes narrow, just a tiny bit, as I speak. Next to me, Mack clears his throat loudly.

"Yeah," Nico chuckles. "Bit hairy out there." He breathes out through pursed lips. "Town's swarming with reporters. Took the long way round and avoided them though." He goes to Nova and sits opposite her. "No one saw me," he says, reaching for her hands.

As the four of us watch, Nova forces a smile on her face. She's a good actress; she looks genuinely pleased. "That's good," she says. "Really good." After a pause, she adds, "Did you get them? The results? Mack said you couldn't email them."

Nico reaches triumphantly into his pocket. He produces a piece of paper and unfolds it, flattening it onto the table with his palm. "You bet I did." He squeezes her hand.

I can almost feel the anger coming from Kole.

He stalks to the other side of the room while he watches.

Taking the seat next to Nico, Tanner rotates the piece of paper and stares at it.

"What does it say?" Nova looks from Tanner to Nico.

Nico shakes his head. "Couldn't make it out. Bunch of numbers and letters in a table."

"Shit." Tanner swipes his fingers through his hair and thumps back in his seat.

"What?" Nova ducks her head to meet his eyes. "What is it, Tanner?"

"It says you're a witch." He runs his index finger down the table. "According to this, you're sixty percent witch. Fire affinity. Witch." He seems stunned. He pushes the paper toward Mack, and Mack examines it.

"That's not possible," Kole growls.

Tanner simply shakes his head.

For a moment, there's silence, then Mack says, "Page one of three." He turns to Nico, his amber eyes flashing. "Where's two and three?"

"Ah…" Nico swallows hard. He reaches for his pocket. All four of us tense. "I couldn't print the rest. Paper jam." He raises his index finger. "*But* I did take screenshots."

He turns his phone over to Tanner. Tan snatches it and pinches the screen to zoom in. "There's a video too. I didn't know what to do with that one, so I recorded it." He leans over and swipes the screen. "There." He looks around at the rest of us. "Doesn't mean anything to me but I thought it might be important…"

"By the moon," Tanner breathes out hard. He stands up then sits down again. "Holy hell, Mack."

Mack slams the paper down and tilts his head to watch the video. I want to do the same, but I refuse to take my eyes off Nico, and Kole clearly feels the same.

"It's changing." Tanner turns the phone and shows it to Nova. "Your DNA is changing." He waggles his finger at the phone. "Those two screenshots, and the printed page, they're tests taken over three days. Her DNA begins twenty percent witch, then forty, then sixty." He looks up at Mack. "The video shows her blood under a microscope. You can literally see it changing."

"Does that happen?" Nova asks. "I mean, is this something that usually happens?"

Mack shakes his head. "No. It's not."

Nova looks stunned. Her face has drained of its color. She presses her palms to the table and breathes out steadily. Nico reaches for her, notices the mark on her neck, and says, "Nova? What happened?" But when he brushes her skin, she flinches.

Nico frowns. "Hey, it's okay. This is good news, right?" He looks at the rest of us. "This is the proof you needed."

Slowly, Kole walks over and places a hand on Nova's shoulder. Tanner has pocketed Nico's phone. Nova pulls the piece of paper toward her and then slides out of her seat as Kole takes her place.

Nico laughs nervously, then swallows hard. "What's going on, guys?" He laughs again. "This is good. Right? Good news?"

"Did you give these tests to anyone else?" Mack asks. I position myself next to him so that Nico is hemmed in. Surrounded.

"No." He frowns. "Of course, not. Why would I?"

Fire flickers in my gut. "Because you're a fucking spy," I spit, unable to contain my fury any longer.

Nico opens his mouth to speak. Before he can, Mack hits him with the restraints. Together, we mutter an incantation to bind Nico's wrists behind his back. As they're jerked backward, he yelps. He tries to shift. His shoulders unlock, and his limbs crack, but he can't complete the transformation. We've got him.

As soon as he's bound tightly by our invisible cuffs, Kole puts a hand around Nico's throat and hauls him to his feet. "You're H.E.L.," he says. "Don't deny it."

Nico's eyes widen. He looks at Nova. A silent tear falls down her cheek.

16

NOVA

Watching the guys surround Nico, I shake from head to toe. One tear falls, then another, then another.

I turn away and look up at the ceiling because I can't bear to look at him. A few hours ago, he was the brother I thought I'd never see again. Now he's a traitor. The veneer has slipped and all I see is betrayal.

"I can explain," Nico splutters. "It's complicated, but I can explain."

"Then explain." I whirl around, a rush of fire sweeping from my belly to my throat. "Tell me who you are." I push past the others. Kole spins Nico around and holds him by the shoulders. He's taller than me, but I rise and stare at him as I spit, "Who are you? Are you Sam? Are you my brother?"

Nico stares at me for a moment. I almost expect him to smirk, but he doesn't. "Yes," he says. "I am."

"Nova, you know he's lying." Luther's fingers are splayed. Fire crackles in his palms. The heat in the room is building.

I narrow my eyes and stare into Nico's face. "Are you my brother?" I ask him again.

"Yes," he says, "I am."

But this time, his words feel different. There's something in his eyes that wasn't there before. "You're lying," I say quietly. "I can see it."

"I'm your brother. I have the scars." He flexes his shoulders like he's trying to pull his arms forward. "The mark on my wrist." But it's as if he's repeating a rehearsed script.

"You're lying." I look at Tanner. "He's lying."

Tanner slips his hand into mine. "Yes, he is, Little Star."

A volcano of heat erupts in my belly. I'm closing my eyes, pushing it down, trying to focus when the ground shakes. The kitchen rattles. Cups fall from shelves. Plates smash. A mirror drops and shatters into a million pieces.

I look at my hands. Was that me?

Nico's eyes are wide and frightened. Beads of sweat break out on his forehead. The room is airless. Like a summer's day before a storm. Full to the top with a cloying heat that squeezes my lungs.

"That wasn't me." My palms are empty.

Luther's are too now. He rushes to the doors. Lights have appeared in the trees. A kaleidoscope of different colors. Blue, green, white.

"The Bureau. They're here." Mack throws an arm in front of me to shield me from the windows. "Fucking Tom. Lied through his teeth."

When the mansion shakes again, Kole hunches over my head, curling his body around mine. "They broke the shield. They're in the woods."

The windows shatter. Glass falls. The sound is deafening. Heat rushes from the room, replaced by icy cold.

Mack throws Nico to the ground and ties an invisible chain around his ankle, jerking him toward the table. He tugs against it but can't move.

Together, Luther and Mack take the stone steps and run toward the trees. Kole follows them. Luther creates a wall of fire, separating them from whatever's coming.

Tanner clutches my hand. "Wait here. Hide." He kisses my forehead. "Wait here." Then he strides out to join the others.

I stand on the top step watching as they form a line. All four of them. For a long moment, everything is quiet. Then a noise, like thunder, vibrates in the air. A chopper flies over The Hollow. A voice, tinny and loud, shouts, "Luther Ross, Kole Trajan, Tanner Booth, Rhone Mackenzie, we know who you are, and we know you're hiding the girl. Hand her over, and then we can talk."

Hearing the boys' full names like that fills me with a strange tugging warmth. They look at each other but stand firm. Tanner raises his hand. Beads of moisture float up from the grass and form a swirling ball. Luther opens his palms and flicks fire into them.

Mack stretches his arms out to his sides. Air swirls around him, whipping leaves up from the floor. I never knew he had an affinity too. I always thought he was just a shifter, but now it makes complete sense; he is exactly like air. Sometimes soothing, sometimes rough. Steady. Always there.

When I look at Kole, my blood runs cold. His fingers are splayed. His head tilted back. The trees in front of him shake. Leaves and branches quiver. The ground begins to rumble.

"Nova," Nico pleads. "Let me go."

I turn to him. Fire flashes in my eyes. I see it reflected in his.

"Please, let me go. If the Bureau finds me here, it'll be worse for you. They'll think you kidnapped me. Please, let me go."

I stride slowly over to him. I watch him for a moment, then I turn and walk away.

By the time I reach the others, the lawn outside The Hollow is moving. Like there's an ocean beneath it, trying to break free, it lifts and rises beneath my feet.

The lights in the trees grow closer. Dark figures appear in the undergrowth, staring out at us. I trip and steady myself as a huge tree root breaks free from the earth. At Luther's side, I exchange a firm glance with him. He doesn't tell me to leave. I look at his hands, then copy his stance and bring flames into mine.

"Tom, don't do this," Mack shouts into the trees.

"It's too late for that, Mack," a voice calls back. "Give up the girl. Then we'll talk. I promise."

Mack closes his eyes. "Sorry, Tom, I don't trust your promises anymore." He nods at the others. Then, before I realize what's happening, all hell breaks loose.

Spells hurtle at us from the trees. Agents storm forward. Mack's legs are clamped together with a restraining spell, but Luther breaks it.

I copy Luther, throwing fire to meet spells, but then fire comes back at us in return. Three water mage agents hold hands and send a tsunami of water sweeping toward us. Tanner catches it, tries to stop it, but fails and is swept off his feet.

Turning to Tanner, Kole roars and opens a hole in the earth to swallow the water. His power is different. He's trembling all over. He pulls roots from the earth, forming a barrier around us. Trees fall. The air swirls.

Above our heads, the incessant thunk-thunk-thunk of the chopper never stops.

Cocooned in Kole's roots, Luther and I create a circle of fire so the five of us are completely enclosed.

"Mack, take Nova to the cabin." Luther squeezes Mack's arm. "We'll hold them off here as long as we can, then we'll join you."

Mack's eyes flicker as he looks into Luther's. "Be careful."

"We will." Luther turns to Kole. "Make an opening, let them out back." Then to Tanner, "Can you do something with the river to distract them?"

Tanner nods. Swiftly, he kisses my lips. I kiss him back and squeeze Kole's hand. "I love you both." Then, as something that sounds like an explosion rattles the earth, Kole opens a door in the roots so Mack and I can escape.

We round the corner of the house just as Tanner pulls a huge wave of water from the river and sends it hurtling toward the agents in the trees.

Mack shifts while he's running. His clothes fall in shreds at his feet. He pauses, dips his head so I can climb onto Snow's back, then keeps running.

Burying my hands in his fur, I hold on tight. I press my face into his shoulder and squeeze my thighs around his huge, bulky body. He roars loudly. Something whizzes past us. A spell. Bright blue.

Snow starts to limp. I look down and see a flash of blood on his leg.

"Snow, you're hurt…" I move my arms forward toward his neck. He groans but doesn't stop running.

By the time we reach the outskirts of town, he's slowing down.

The noise of the chopper and the fighting is becoming distant. Snow huffs hard, struggling to catch his breath. "Stop," I tell him. "Stop here."

He does as I ask, and I slide down from his back. His leg is bleeding, the fur matted. Snow leans into my chest. He makes a noise that rattles through me. I press myself to him. "Can you keep moving?" I ask, stroking his face.

Snow dips his head to answer me.

"Okay, but I'm walking." I tilt my head. "And I won't take no for an answer."

17

TANNER

When we arrive at the cabin, we find Mack stretched out on the couch, pants rolled up, and Nova bent over his leg trying to clean a nasty-as-hell spell burn.

"Lucky, I grabbed this on the way out." I hold up my medical bag. The only thing I managed to take from the carnage of our final few moments in The Hollow.

"What happened?" Nova rushes over to us. "Are you three alright?"

"We couldn't fight them off any longer," Kole says, adrenaline making his voice grate like sandpaper on his tongue. He shudders. The veins in his arms are bulging.

"Nico?" Nova asks, concern shimmering around her—even if she doesn't want it to.

Kole shakes his head. "By the time we got inside, he was gone."

I interrupt, looking at Mack. "We had to leave, Mack. I'm sorry. I don't know what they'll do to the place."

"You think I care about that?" he asks, pushing himself up onto his elbows. "As long as you all are alright."

"We're fine," Luther says before promptly wobbling on the spot.

I tuck his arm around my shoulders and steady him. Depositing him in an armchair, I fetch him some water. "You need to get your core temp down." I nod for him to drink it.

Luther pulls off his shirt. Beads of sweat cling to his skin. He leans forward onto his knees and drinks the whole glass in one swig. I refill it and gesture for him to drink another.

"We weren't followed," he tells Mack, panting, "Borrowed a car. Masked it."

Mack nods. Masking is a restricted incantation—for use by police and SDB only. At this point, however, his and Luther's careers are pretty much down the tube anyway.

"Cell phones?" Mack asks, wincing as I sit on the coffee table and start to examine his leg.

"Did ours in the car," Luther replies. "Yours?"

Mack moves his gaze to the two cells sitting next to me. "Done."

"Good." Luther holds out his glass for a refill and I oblige. He drinks it quickly, wipes his mouth, then says, "Then we just have one thing left to hide." He raises his eyes to the ceiling. "This place."

"Luther…" Mack tries to sit up, but I put my hand on his knee and shake my head at him; the spell burn is deep and nasty. Blackened flesh around the edges of the burn shows an infection will take hold if it's not cleaned up properly. "We don't have the power—"

"Between the four of us, we can do it." Luther glances at Kole, who's still simmering with whatever the hell effect Nova's blood had on him.

"No." Mack sounds more like Snow than himself. His eyes flash. "We can't."

Clearing her throat, as if she's afraid to interrupt, Nova says, "Isn't that what you did to The Hollow? Why is the cabin different?"

"We only shielded The Hollow," I explain gently. "Shielding creates a force field. Like an invisible wall that people can't cross. Masking is different. It's literally a case of making it look like something doesn't exist anymore."

"It'll give off too much energy." Mack winces and sucks his cheeks in as I start cleaning his leg. "The Bureau will be looking for spell signatures. They'll see it."

"So, we cast a wider area. Wide enough that it'll take them forever to pinpoint the cabin. Or at least long enough for us to figure out our next move." Luther's temperature is returning to normal. He shivers violently and pulls his shirt back on. I can't be certain, but I'm sure I noticed Nova watching as he moved across the room shirtless.

Mack is shaking his head, still against the idea, when Kole says, "We can do it, Mack. You saw what I did back there. I'm still—"

"High?" Mack says, raising his eyebrows.

Kole's eyes darken. "No. It's different from that." He pauses, clearly not able or willing to get into whatever is going on in his head and body since he sunk his teeth into our girl. "My powers have quadrupled. I'm strong. And if we add Nova…"

"Nova?" I ask, spreading thick anti-burn gel onto Mack's leg.

"She has power. We've seen it. With her, we can mask the cabin, the woods, the lake, all of it." Kole looks at Luther.

Luther nods in agreement.

For a moment, I feel like I've stepped back in time. Like I'm witnessing what these two must have been like as students of Mack's; pushing the boundaries, ganging up on him when they felt they knew better.

"Mack—" Nova is sitting on the arm of the couch near Mack's feet. She rubs his ankle. "If I can help, let me. It shouldn't be up to you three to keep me safe. I'm part of this too, and not just as some precious thing you need to protect. If the prophecy's right, I've got more power inside me than the four of you combined. Even with Kole in Hulk mode." Her eyes flicker and a smile dances on her lips. Glancing at Kole, she adds, "Green? Trees? Nature? Hulk?" She laughs at herself. "Okay, bad joke." Then she returns to Mack and in a more serious tone says, "Seriously. Let me help."

"Why don't we put it to a vote?" I ask, winding a bandage around Mack's leg. "All those in favor of trying to mask this place, with Nova's help, raise your hands."

Kole, Luther, Nova, and I all raise our arms into the air.

Mack raises two, but I pull one back down. "Snow doesn't get a separate vote."

"That's decided then." Nova stands up and puts her hands on her hips. "What next?"

At the kitchen table, Luther spreads out a map of the cabin and the surrounding area. He draws a big red cross to indicate the cabin's position. "We'll need to separate. Head out to the furthest edge of the boundary, then cast the incantation." He looks at each of us in turn. "We'll have to be exact. To the second. Each of us casts at exactly the right time. Thirty-second intervals to form the mask."

"How do we...?" Nova rubs her forearms. "I've only ever created flames. I've never *cast* any spells or incantations."

Moving closer to her, Luther puts his hand flat on her stomach, locking eyes with her. Nova flinches, but he doesn't take it away.

"You feel it here," he says, applying a little pressure. "The same as with the flames. Pull the magic down inside your body. Then you speak the incantation. At the same time, you let it flow through you. Picture it flooding your veins, your muscles, your bones, your soul. Let it take over."

Nova's breath hitches in her chest. She lets out a small, "Oh." Her cheeks are flushed.

Luther is staring at her. We've all noticed. When he breaks his gaze, he clears his throat and says, "That's how. That's how you cast."

"Should I practice?" she asks.

"Sure." Luther puts the pen firmly on the map. "Make it fly."

"Fly?" she laughs, then realizes he's not joking.

Putting his hand on her arm, Mack tells her, "Eventually, you'll be able to move things without spells. The elements tie together and influence one another. Fire mages can create currents of hot air and manipulate objects that way. But, for now, try *koda srek vam krae.*"

A little stilted, Nova repeats, "*Koda srek vam krae.*"

Mack nods. "Close your eyes. Do what Luther told you. Then speak the spell."

Smoothing her hands over her top, Nova shakes her arms at her sides. She inhales deeply, flexes her fingers, and closes her eyes. For a moment, she doesn't move. She's completely still. The rhythm of her breath, moving up and down in her chest, is hypnotic. Her skin becomes flushed. A spark flies from her palm. I'm about to tell her to pull the magick back down inside herself when Luther shakes his head at me.

He presses a finger to his lips.

We are all silent.

Finally, she says it: "*Koda srek vam krae*." She opens her eyes slowly. A grin spreads her lips wide. "I did it," she whispers.

In front of her, Luther's pen is floating.

We don't wait until nightfall. Nova practices a few more incantations, then Luther tells us it's time. Following his directions, we separate and spread to our positions. North, South, East, and West, with Nova in the center.

Allowing Nova to walk off into the woods alone feels all kinds of wrong, but she simply flicks a flame into her palm and says firmly, "I'll be fine. I've got this."

When we're in position, we text. Usually, our group chat is for gross gifs, stupid jokes, and the occasional perfunctory message about needing toilet paper or milk. Today, Nova is added to the chat and our messages say simply:

Kole: *Here*

Luther: *Here*

Mack: *Here*

Tanner: *Here*

Nova's dots move on the screen as she types.

Nova: *Lost.*

Just as all our dots are going crazy tapping out responses, she texts back.

Nova: *Joking. Sorry. Here.*

I chuckle and push my hair from my face. I'd love to see Luther's expression right now, although something tells me he's starting to warm up to our little supernova.

I'm the first to cast. I stretch my arms out to my sides, open the gates in my head, and let the energy of the water beneath the ground and in the air surge through me. I push it down into the basement of my being then—as I say the words—I release it.

The air quivers. There's a flash of bright blue light. A shimmering wall of nothingness forms in front of me. It moves like invisible waves through the air, up and up, forming a dome that stretches up above the trees. It curves out, around the lake, then meets another flash. Green. Kole.

In the distance, barely visible through the trees, there's a third flash. Pure white. Mack. Shifter and air mage.

Then red. Fire. Luther.

I wait. Thirty seconds pass. The second flash of red doesn't come. I stare and stare, as if I might conjure it with my eyes just by wanting it enough. I'm about to look away and check for messages from the others when the trees begin to shiver. The ground vibrates. *Boom.* A burst of burning orange illuminates the sky. It rushes toward me and slams into my blue light with a force that knocks me from my feet.

The mask is formed.

It worked. I check my phone.

Nova: *Did you see that?! MAN, I love spells. Can you teach me some more?*

18

NICO

I keep running until the pain in my feet makes me stop. My paws are bleeding, the pads almost clean scraped off from skidding on the glass in the hallway. I lick them. It doesn't help.

When I shift back, the injury stays with me. I peel off the sneakers Tanner gave me and examine my feet. My soles are raw, and the palms of my hands burn. Sitting with my back against a tree, a few paces back from the side of the road, I put my head in my hands and exhale a long, shaky breath.

I have no idea where Mother and Ragnor are staying now. Since the fire at the hotel, they must have needed a new place to hide. But no one thought it necessary to share the location with me.

I don't even have a number to call.

I reel back through my memory. Try to remember places we've met before. Places Ragnor has mentioned. There was a big old house somewhere on the outskirts of Solleville where Mother took me there once when I was small. It had big black iron gates and a sweeping driveway. But it's too far from here; with my injured feet, I'll never make it.

So, stumbling to my feet, I head for my apartment instead. I have a small place here in the city. A penthouse with views over the whole of Red Rock.

The thought of being surrounded by my own things, safe with my own thoughts and actions, makes me suddenly tearful.

Stumbling to my feet, I wince as I begin to walk. It will take at least three hours to travel the distance between Phoenix Falls and the Red Rock apartment. Less if I shift, but I'm not sure I can handle the pain. At least in sneakers, my feet won't take further damage.

So, I walk. Slowly.

When cars pass, I duck back into the shadow of the trees. At the tunnel, I keep my head down and press against the curved concrete wall every time a vehicle roars through.

Six black SUVs tear past in convoy. Doesn't take a genius to figure out they're SDB and headed for the chaos in Phoenix Falls.

By the time I reach the outskirts of the city, my head is pounding. The sights and sounds of the busy streets make my ears buzz. Passing a street vendor selling Red Rock merchandise, I wait until they're not looking then swipe a large hoodie, pull it over my clothes, and jerk the hood up to obscure my face.

The final twenty minutes of the journey to the apartment are torturous. When I reach it, I approach the front desk. The doorman, Freddie, eyes me up and down. "Geez, Nico, you look like crap. You okay, man?"

I laugh and shrug my shoulders. "Rough few nights."

"Not hanging out at *Spine* again, are you?" Freddie whistles through his front teeth. I haven't frequented the dark and depraved *Spine* nightclub for months, but I nod and give him a sheepish smile.

Tapping his nose with his index finger, Freddie says, "Don't worry, boss, it'll stay between you and me."

"Thanks, Fred." I make a show of patting down my hoodie. "Seem to have lost my keycard. Can you order me another?"

Freddie nods and taps his keyboard. "Done. Canceled the old one too." He reaches into a drawer beneath the desk. "Here. Use this 'til the new card arrives."

As I take it from him, he noticed my reddened palms and raises his eyebrows. "Shit, Nico. You do the fire-play room again?"

I shove my hands, and the card, into my pockets.

After a pause, Freddie lowers his voice and adds, "Want to share any gruesome details? Did you see that gal again? The one with the red hair?"

"Actually, Fred do you mind if I...?" I look toward the elevator. "I'm beat."

Freddie looks disappointed. He's the kind of guy who'd never have the balls to visit a place like *Spine*, but who likes to get off on hearing what other people get up to there.

"Tomorrow," I promise him. "I'll bring you coffee and give you *all* the details." When I reach the elevator, I flash him a true Nico Varlac smile and add, "Tall latte, three sugars, and a donut. Am I right?"

Freddie slaps the desk and makes a *ho ho* sound like Santa Claus. "Sure thing, Nico. See you tomorrow, buddy."

In the elevator, I lean back against the wall and allow myself to breathe. The smile drops from my lips. I look at my hands. They're trembling.

Finally, inside, I go straight to the bathroom and pull off my clothes. I stand naked under the shower. When it runs hot, it scalds the fragile skin on my feet and hands. So, I turn the temperature down and stand beneath a stream of ice-cold water for a very long time.

Since the fire at the hotel, escaping with Nova, and ending up back at The Hollow, I haven't allowed myself to think about it in any kind of detail. I tried to block out the sound and smell of my burning flesh. The sight of Eve standing above me, taking her time to create a convincing pattern of burns that would convince Nova I was her brother Sam.

I tried not to see my mother's face as she watched, or the glint in Ragnor's eyes—anticipation rather than sympathy.

But now it bombards me. The events of the past few days barrel through me and knock me down to the floor. I tuck my knees under my chin, wrap my arms around them, and try to feel clean.

When I finally drag myself to my feet and climb out, wrapping a soft white towel around my waist, I go to the living room, close the electric blinds, and turn on the TV.

Almost every news channel shows the same thing: The Hollow surrounded by SDB agents, trees burning, roots bursting from the ground. Mounds of earth, deep black trenches.

And then they cut to the footage of Nova. She's standing next to Luther, fire in her hands. Spell blasts bounce off the small shield they've formed around themselves. There's smoke. Lots of smoke. Kole hauls tree roots from the earth and creates a cocoon around the five of them. A wall of fire surrounds the roots. Then a huge wave of water rips across The Hollow's grounds, coming from the river. When the smoke and the water clears, Nova and Mack are gone.

Her picture appears on the screen. One shows her with auburn hair. The other is a freeze-frame of the silver-haired Nova I know.

I move closer.

As I'm staring at her face, the door buzzes. I breathe out heavily as I stand.

"Yes, Fred?" I speak into the camera on the wall.

Freddie's eyes dart to something off-camera. When they return to me, he says, "Sorry, Nico. I know you said you were heading straight to bed, but there's a woman here who says she's your mother? And she's very insistent that I let her up."

A chill drips down my spine. "Alright, Freddie. Let her up."

I wait, staring into the empty hallway. When the elevator opens, my blood runs cold. Mother isn't inside; it's Eve who steps out and smiles at me.

Practically floating toward me, Eve coos, "Nico, I'm so relieved you're safe."

My mouth is dry. I can't speak. The scars on my chest and back burn when she looks at them. I step aside and she brushes past me into the room. There's no one with her. She's alone.

"We saw what was happening on the news. Your father asked me to retrieve you. By the time I got there, you'd already left."

I frown. Ragnor asked her to get me out? For a brief moment, my heart swells at the thought he cared enough to send someone to rescue me. Then reality punches me in the gut. He didn't care about my safety; he simply wanted to make sure I wasn't captured by the SDB.

"They had me in restraints, but when the SDB broke through the shield the restraint spell failed and I ran. I didn't know where to find you all, so I came back here—"

"Sensible." Eve traces a finger over my bicep. "Very sensible." She glances at the TV. "Our fire bird made quite the mess, didn't she?"

I nod.

"Do you know where they took her?"

I swallow hard and pinch the bridge of my nose. I heard them talking about a cabin. The words are on the tip of my tongue but, for some reason, I can't bring myself to say them. Something deep in my gut, the first real instinct of my own that I've had in years, tells me to stay quiet. I meet Eve's eyes and hold my nerve. "No," I tell her. "They just ran."

Eve blinks at me. She ticks her head to the side. Then she smiles. "No matter. We'll find her again." She slips her hand into mine. "And now, my darling, it's time to return you to your father."

19

KOLE

TWO DAYS LATER

Mack and Luther leave at sunset. The mask is still holding, and the SDB hasn't found us yet. But that doesn't mean it's time to get complacent. So, they wait until the sun goes down then go to meet Rev at the barrier.

If it was up to me, we'd have made do with the clothes on our backs and the fish Snow and Tanner have been catching from the lake. But they're not just meeting Rev for clothes and food supplies; they're meeting her for news of what's going on in town.

For the last forty-eight hours, Nova's and our mugshots have been blasted over every social media channel and TV station—along with speculation that we're behind H.E.L. itself—but *actual* news about how close the Bureau is to locating us? That's impossible to find.

Mack thinks something strange is going on—that if they really wanted to track us down, they'd have done it by now. If Luther agrees, he hasn't said as much. But then, he hasn't said much at all since we got here. Whether he's pissed that we're in *his* cabin, or just pissed that we're in his cabin with Nova, I can't work out.

"You still in Hulk mode?" Tanner interrupts my brooding by giving me a light punch on the arm.

If he knew the half of how I'm feeling… it's waned over the past two days, but I still feel wired. It doesn't help that we're in a forest, surrounded by trees and earth and plants. All moving and pulsing, their energy pressing down on the cabin.

I look at Nova. She's leaning on the counter. Her hair is scraped back, her neck on display, her ass jutting out the bottom of Luther's spare tee.

A rumble, like thunder, drips through me. "Maybe we should test it." In one swift movement, I sweep her into my arms and pick her up. She shrieks delightfully and laughs as I bounce her up and down.

"That proves nothing." Tanner rolls his eyes. "You could do that before."

"Then why didn't you?" Nova coos, clenching her thighs around my waist. "I like it up here."

"Is that so?" I rest her on the counter for a moment then say, "In which case I think you'll love it up here." I pick her up again, but this time I turn her so she's facing away from me then lift her higher, and higher until she's on my shoulders.

Nova wobbles, steadies her hands on my head and clamps my neck with her legs. "Kole, no way, put me down."

"If you say so, Little Star."

Tanner stands back and watches with amusement as I lower Nova gently back to the counter.

When I look at him, there's a sparkle in his eyes. He raises an eyebrow at me. "You think you could hold her upside down?" he asks, grinning as his eyes follow a path from her legs to her panties peeking out from beneath the hem of the tee. Deliciously dark and lacey.

Nova shakes her head. "Oh, hell no." She jumps down from the counter, laughing, and tears across the living room.

The sound of her screeching as Tanner hooks his arms around her waist, and the thud of her heartbeat in my veins makes me instantly hard.

She breaks away from Tanner, because he lets her, and laughs, but she's backed herself into the corner of the room.

In a pincer movement, we close in on her. Tanner looks at me, bolts for her, then stops as she runs headfirst into my chest.

"Kole... don't." But she's still laughing.

As I pick her up, she thumps my arms, squirming. I let her wrestle me then, over her shoulder, motion for Tanner to come help.

As if he knows exactly what I'm planning, he pins her arms

behind her back and holds her upper half against his chest, supporting her weight while I squat down and hook her legs around my neck.

Nova wriggles again. "You'll drop me!"

"No, Little Star, I won't." I'm supporting her back with my arms and hands, her legs with my shoulders. "As long as you keep very still." I smile at her as I lower my head and kiss the inside of her thigh.

Slowly, I move my lips up toward her panties. She tilts her hips, like she's trying to get closer, but I move my mouth to her other thigh and start all over again.

Watching me, Tanner edges the three of us backward and leans on the arm of the couch. I move with him, as Tanner lowers Nova so she's tilted head-down.

With one arm still holding her against his chest, Tanner slips his free hand beneath her shirt and pulls it up to expose her breasts. She's braless and her nipples are already hard.

Arousal tugs at my dick as I watch her start to play with them. She uses Tanner's mouth to moisten her fingers, then pinches her nipples, tweaks them, massages them.

I return to the very top of her thigh and start working my tongue along her skin, still not touching her pussy, leaving her panties painfully in place.

"Stop... teasing... me," she pleads breathlessly.

I scrape my teeth along her leg. From her knee all the way up to her damp panties.

"Kole," Tanner drawls out in a warning.

"I won't bite," I promise him.

Expertly, I pull her underwear to one side with my mouth. Then I sweep my tongue over her clit and make fierce circles around it.

Nova tries to keep still, but when she starts keening and grinding against my mouth, I raise my head, her taste slick on my lips.

I nod at Tanner, and he lifts Nova into my arms so I can lower her down my body. Reaching beneath her ass, Tanner unfastens my jeans and pulls them over my hips.

"Commando?" he asks, his hands skimming my erection. He smiles, drops his own pants, and says, "Same." With an impish grin, he attempts to high-five me. Despite myself, I laugh and slap his palm with mine.

Nova gives us a look that's half-amusement and half get-the-heck-on-with-it, but Tanner's still grinning so I raise my eyebrows at him and gesture to the waistband of Nova's panties. "Take these off her," I command. Immediately, Tanner tears them from Nova's hips. His arms ripple as he whips them away. Swimmer's arms, tanned and toned.

Nova kisses my shoulder, running her fingers over my inked upper arms. "You don't want to put me down?"

"I'm not done with you yet, Little Star." I kiss her and pull her closer to my body.

Behind her, Tanner plants a line of kisses down her spine. Our fingers meet on her clit. He moves his to her pussy, and the shape she makes with her mouth tells me he's put one inside her.

Leaving one arm around my neck, Nova lowers her free hand, searching for the tip of my cock. When she finds it, she grips me tight and tries to edge herself toward my hips.

"I want you both," she says.

I cock my head.

"In the same place." She reaches behind her, brings Tanner's lips to her mouth and kisses him.

As their lips lock, I feel Tanner's hand on my dick. He holds our shafts together, grasps them both, and works his fist back and forth.

I groan into Nova's chest.

Breaking their kiss, Tanner asks, "Do you think she can take two cocks?" His eyes are smiling.

"I'm not sure." I bite my lower lip as a moan escapes Nova's mouth.

"Yes. Please. I need you both."

I nod at Tanner. He helps me ease Nova's legs open further, so her pussy stretches to welcome us. As I hold her, he positions our tips at her entrance.

"Relax," he whispers. Then, in tandem, we ease our way in as I slowly ease her down onto us both.

Nova's eyes widen as we fill her up. She smiles, gloriously happy as she lowers her weight onto us more.

When we're all the way in, she sighs. I catch Tanner's eyes. They're clouded with arousal. He puts his hands on my waist. His cock twitches, and the sensation of it pulsing against mine makes me grab his hair and pull him to my lips.

For years, Tanner and I have given each other what we need when we need it. But now, with Nova between us, it's like the pieces of our relationship have fallen into place.

I could never make sense of what he was to me. It was so mixed up with the way we came into each other's lives that I couldn't distill it into what was real and what was just two lost souls trying to heal.

In this moment, I know it was meant to be this way. We were meant to find each other so we could find Nova, and so we could end up here. With her.

Watching us, Nova eases herself up using my shoulders as leverage, then slowly slides back down. She steals Tanner's lips from mine, then hungrily kisses me too.

We rock up inside her, syncing the rhythm of our hips. I push Nova's damp hair from her cheeks to kiss the flushed pinkness.

Her hair is still tied back. Her neck is exposed and I can see the bruise I left in the ballroom is fading. Tanner catches me looking and, before I realize what he's about to do, he slams his hand around my throat.

"Don't," he growls.

The sudden role reversal and the iron in his voice makes me grunt with pleasure. Nova shouts, "Yes, yes, yes!" as she grinds down onto our cocks.

Her walls start to flutter. Tanner slots his hand between us and finds her clit.

"Tanner! Fuck!" she yells, her nails scratching over my back.

As an orgasm explodes through her, she goes stiff in our arms, back arched. Her skin glowing. Heat clamps around my cock, pressing it against Tanner's as we continue to pump into her.

I feel him get harder. He yells, "Holy hell, Nova!" but doesn't take his hand from my throat.

When his cum fills her up, coating my shaft and his, I bite his hand. Not hard enough to draw blood. Just enough to release the pressure in my jaw.

I throw my head back and roar as I come. The orgasm batters my body like a fierce storm. Shaking, I sink to the floor.

Nova falls back into Tanner's embrace while he lowers her feet back to the ground. She stands, turns to press herself against him, and kisses his chest.

Together, they offer me their hands and pull me to my feet. Nova looks at my body appreciatively, then strokes my beard and brushes her lips against mine.

For a long moment, we kiss, stroke, and hold each other. The three of us.

Then Nova throws her hand over her mouth and yawns. "Sorry," she laughs, shaking her head. "I'm suddenly exhausted."

Catching her yawn, Tanner says, "Me too," and casts his eyes to the ceiling. "Bed?" he asks me.

I find my jeans and pull them back on. My teeth still itch with the need for Nova's skin. The hunger hasn't come, but the knowledge it might makes me tell the two of them to go ahead and rest. "I'll stay up and wait for the others." I kiss Nova's forehead. "Hopefully Rev packaged you some new underwear." I squeeze her ass playfully. I'd be perfectly happy if she never wore underwear again, but I admit it's not the most practical choice given our circumstances.

"Come to bed as soon as they're back." She runs her hand down my chest. Then she trots ahead of Tanner so he can chase her upstairs. He pauses on the bottom step and looks back at me.

"You alright?" he mouths.

I nod solemnly. I'm alright. I'm all *kinds* of *al*right. But I know I can't let myself taste her again. Once, I was lucky. I might not be so lucky a second time around.

20

NICO

W e've been at Ragnor's house in Solleville for two days. I haven't seen him yet, but Mother came to me straight away. She had no idea Eve had been sent to fetch me and was furious that Eve and Ragnor went behind her back. But she's pleased I'm here; finally in the fold.

For two days I've been moving around the house trying to get a hold on what's happening. The place is a hive of activity since H.E.L. has taken it over; wolves and other supers with the League's insignia tattooed on their backs swarm the building. No one seems to have noticed or care that *Nico Varlac* is suddenly in their midst. At first, I thought Ragnor might have finally told them I'm his son. But when a big thick-necked werewolf named Andre asked me how long I'd been working undercover, and how I got introduced to the League, I realized I was wrong.

Sitting outside under the stars, watching the lights of the house flicker as silhouettes pass them, I'm wondering what else I've been wrong about.

When Mother appears across the lawn, the moonlight illuminates the scar on her face. She sits down next to me on a cold stone bench and looks back at the house.

"What's happening in there?" I ask because this is the first time we've been alone together since I got here.

"Ragnor is getting ready," she says quietly.

"Ready for what?" A sickening chill creeps down my spine.

Mother closes her eyes. In a voice that's barely a whisper, she says, "The beginning of the end."

21

NOVA

I try to wait for Kole, but sleep takes over. Tanner is cool against my constantly over-heated body. I curl into him, my back to his chest, my ass cupped by the curve of his hips. His arms are big and strong. Wrapped inside them, I feel safe. Completely safe.

For a while, he strokes me. His hands roam lovingly over my body like he's trying to learn every dip and groove. Commit them to memory. He nuzzles into my neck. His breathing changes to a slower rhythm. I lace my fingers between his.

I'm drifting beneath the surface of sleep when Kole finally comes to join us. He slips into bed on the other side of me, hooks his big heavy leg over mine, and kisses my forehead. *Are you awake, Little Star?*

Without opening my eyes, I tell him, *No. I'm sleeping.*

He brushes my lips with his thumb, lightly pinching the spot where I'm trying to fight a smile. I pull him toward me. It's pitch dark. Unable to see him, my other senses are heightened. I breathe in his scent. My pulse quickens. I can feel it in my neck.

I slide my hands down his body and hum a little as he does the same. His cock is hard, pressing against me. I find his mouth, steal a kiss, pull his hair loose from its elastic, and run my fingers through it.

Will you give yourself to me, Little Star?

The question sends a lightning bolt of arousal to my core. My entire body pulsates. I reach for him hungrily.

Is it safe? I ask, already tilting my head so my neck is exposed.

It shouldn't be. Kole draws a line with his finger from my ear to my chest. *It should send me wild with hunger, but something has changed. Something is different.*

SOMETHING IS COMING.

The voice is loud. It startles us both. I grip Kole's shoulders while my heart beats fast. *Did you hear that?*

He cups my face in his hands.

SOMETHING IS COMING.

He kisses me. His teeth pull on my lower lip. Then he grabs my hair, leans in, and sinks his teeth into my neck.

Warmth floods my body. Tidal waves of heat lick my limbs. Ebbing and flowing, sending pulses of desire to tease my skin. I moan and lean into the pain. Something hot trickles down my neck. Kole groans while he's lapping at me, sucking, pulling me closer.

There are hands on my waist. Two sets of hands. I hear Tanner's voice but it's distant. Something is trying to pull me away from Kole, but I hook my arms around his neck and latch on tight. I will not leave him. I'm his. He's mine. My teeth graze his shoulder. I could taste him too, then we'd have each other. Inside.

FIND THE WOLF.

The voice is louder now. Hissing. Pummeling my skull from the inside out.

FIND THE WOLF.

A muffled cry escapes Kole's mouth. The pressure on my neck changes. Then it's no longer darkness I see.

There are lights. Bright lights. A woman is screaming, giving birth. A baby is lifted into a father's arms. The father's face is blurred, but he has blond hair. Almost white. He turns away from the child. His shoulders shake as he sobs. Then the child is older. A boy. Playing with a girl. Her auburn hair shimmers in the sunlight as he chases her around a large oak tree.

FIND THE WOLF.

Fire. Flames. Heat. The boy screams. He wakes in a hospital. Burns all over his body. Nurses slather him with cream while he cries for his sister. "Nova," he sobs. "Where is Nova?"

White light blinds me. I can't see. When it clears, the boy is older. A gangly teenager with dark curly hair. Someone is yelling at him. He's in a basement. Dark, cold. A foot hits his ribs. He falls back and curls into a ball. "We're done. First thing tomorrow, you're out of here." The door at the top of the stairs closes. Darkness swallows the boy whole.

22

TANNER

Mack and Luther haul Kole away from Nova and throw him to the floor. Blood drips down his chin. His eyes are black, his chest rising and falling. The entire room swims in a dancing orange light. On the bed, Nova's skin is glowing. As she sits up, it fades.

Luther turns on the lights.

Nova reaches for me so I sweep her sticky hair from her neck. Congealed blood pools around the bite wound. Next to the first. Bigger and deeper this time.

"What the fuck?" Luther stares at me. "What the fuck happened?"

"I was asleep." I look from Nova to Kole. I felt him come to bed. Felt them touching each other. I was enjoying it, ready for round two. I didn't think for a second—

"The voice." Nova clambers out of the bed. I try to stop her, but she pulls away from me. She walks to Kole and drops to her knees in front of him.

Luther moves to pull her away, but Mack holds up his hand. "Wait," he says, studying the pair of them.

"The voice… did you hear it?" She runs her thumb along Kole's lips.

"I heard it." Kole nods at her.

"Did you see?" she asks. He looks at her neck. His entire body shudders. Outside, the sound of a tree falling makes us all jump.

"I saw."

Kole staggers to his feet, pulling Nova up with him. "Tell them," he says to her, pressing her into Mack's arms. "I need…" He pauses. "Tell them."

Then he heads for the stairs and disappears. Immediately, Luther jogs after him. "Kole," he shouts. The front door slams.

Mack ushers Nova to the bed and sits her down. I fetch my bag and start pulling out the disinfectant.

"What did you see?" Mack asks her gently.

Nova closes her eyes. Her eyelids twitch like, whatever it is, she's still seeing it. When she opens them, she says, "Sam. I saw Sam. Exactly like Sarah said. His mother dying, him and me…" She frowns and pinches the bridge of her nose. "So much of it," she says. "His life, but in miniature snippets." She looks at

Mack. "And the voice. I heard it again. It said, '*Find the Wolf.*'" She reaches for Mack's hands and clasps them between his, her shoulders shaking as a shiver rocks her body.

I grab a blanket and wrap it around her. "Did you see where he is now?" I ask.

"No. I saw him in a basement. He was maybe sixteen years old. Someone was being cruel to him. Very cruel. They told him he had to leave." She pulls the blanket closer. "That was the last thing I saw."

While I finish fixing up Nova's damaged throat, Mack goes to find Kole to see if he saw the same thing Nova did.

"I'm sorry." Her fingers go to her throat.

"Did you want him to?" I ask, pulling her back into my arms as we lean onto the pillows.

"Yes." She's sitting between my legs, stroking my forearm. "I *needed* him to." She tilts her head but winces a little at the sensation. "Is it the blood bond?"

I stroke her hair and kiss her forehead. "Probably."

"And is that why Kole doesn't turn? Like he did before? After the red room?"

I squeeze her tight but don't answer; the truth is I have no idea. Nothing about this makes sense.

"My blood makes his powers stronger," she mutters, glancing toward the window and the swaying trees.

"Yes."

"He saw what I saw." She leans into my chest, then whispers, "We have to find him, Tanner. The voice told us to. The same voice I heard when I came to Phoenix Falls. We *have* to find Sam."

"Did the voice say why?"

Nova clicks her tongue. "No. But Sam's part of this." Her body goes limp as she fights back a yawn. "I know he is. We have to find him," she repeats before giving in to sleep.

In the morning, I leave Nova sleeping and go to make coffee. The others are all splayed out on couches in the living room. Except for Luther, who's awake in the armchair.

He stalks over to help me, looking like he hasn't slept at all.

"I see Rev came through with the supplies," I say, opening the cupboard to find sugar, coffee, and a bunch of breakfast foods.

"She did." He folds his arms and leans back on the countertop.

"What's happening in town?"

"Nothing good." Luther sets out five mugs. "SDB have disappeared."

"And that's not a good thing?" I give him the side-eye.

"No. It means they're regrouping, or that they know something we don't."

"What else?" I drink down a glass of water, then fill another for Nova.

"Rev said everyone is on edge. People are behaving strangely. Getting into fights. Spells going wrong." Luther rubs the back of his neck.

"Maybe because you and Mack aren't around—"

"Seems bigger than that," Luther says gruffly. "According to Rev."

"What about Sarah?" I pour coffee into the mugs, adding cream and sugar for Nova.

"She's going to stay with Rev a while longer."

I look over at Kole. "Is he okay?"

"He's okay." Luther breathes out hard. "Shouldn't have been so fucking dumb. But he's okay."

I take a sip from my mug, then tell Luther what Nova said about her vision. He nods as I retell the story.

"Kole saw the same thing."

"So, whatever happens next, we need to find Sam?" I ask.

Luther swipes his palm over his closely shaved hair. "Maybe." He picks up his coffee. The others are stirring. "We'll go check the perimeter. Come down when she's awake. We'll all talk." He flicks his eyes over to a large black duffel near the door. "Fresh clothes are in there."

I pat his arm, give him a grateful look, then head back to Nova.

She's waiting for me, legs tucked up underneath her, still wearing Luther's tee from yesterday. I put the bag down at the foot of the bed. "Rev sent coffee and clothes," I tell her, handing over a mug.

Downstairs, the front door clunks shut as Mack, Kole, and Luther head out for a morning check on the concealment spell.

She smiles, but her fingers are bothering the mark on her neck. When she notices me watching, she stops and puts down the mug. "Come here," she curls her finger at me.

I flop down on the bed, leaving my coffee on the nightstand.

"I'm sorry." She meets my eyes. "I know you're worried, and I'm sorry. But I'm okay."

Sincerity comes off her in waves. Sincerity and love. It tickles my skin, warming, like a summer breeze. I kiss her passionately on the lips. "Don't apologize to me. I just want you to be safe."

Nova strokes my face, then smiles and tugs Luther's shirt off over her head. In the pale morning light, her breasts are delicious. My cock instantly pays attention.

"I told Luther we'd go talk about—" She steals the words from my mouth with her tongue.

"Make love to me first." She wriggles underneath me, holding my hips with her thighs.

I press my erection against her, and she slips my boxers down.

I meet her gaze as I slide inside her. She sighs and wraps her arms around my neck, holding me close as I move slowly in and out.

For a long time, we kiss and fuck. Slowly and lovingly, our hands and tongues are searching each other's bodies. When we come, it's like a rainstorm. Steady but hard. Nova's back arches, her muscles tense. She quivers against me, her walls twitching until I come too.

I stay inside her for as long as I can, then finally roll over next to her.

We're lying, quietly tangled up in each other, when I find myself saying, "I think Nico wanted you to know he was lying." I kiss her stomach and look up at her. She strokes my hair. "What do you mean?"

"I don't know why. I've been trying to figure it out." I push my fingers through my hair. "It was like he dropped his mask."

"Why would he do that? Why would he want me to know?" She

turns onto her side and leans up on her elbow as I lie back next to her.

I sigh and shake my head. "No idea, Little Star. Maybe a kindness? Maybe just game playing?" I stroke her arm, smoothing her scar with my palm, then move my fingers to the mark on her neck. "I just thought you should know."

Nova closes her eyes and presses her forehead to mine. I lean in and kiss the bruise left by Kole's teeth. "Did it hurt?" I ask softly.

"A little," she sighs, "but also not at all." She lays back and lets me pepper her throat with kisses. "Will he be okay? Will it fade? The... power?"

I sweep her hair up away from her neck and turn her head to the side so that I can kiss the spot beneath her ear. "I don't know."

"Is it dangerous for him?"

"I don't know." I kiss her again. My headache has finally gone. I pause with my hands on her waist. "Nova..." I know what I'm about to say, and I know it's a bad idea, but I also know it's the only way—the only *quick* way—to do what she's convinced needs to be done.

"Mmmm," she sighs and taps her neck. "Don't stop."

"Nova..." I sit up. She realizes I'm serious and sits up too, pulling the sheet around her. "I can find Sam."

"The way you found me and Kole?" A brightness flickers in Nova's eyes. "You really think you can do it?"

I nod. "I know I can." I glance at her cell phone, next to her mug on the nightstand. "Open up the photo Luther gave you—of you and Sam. We'll do it now."

"Now?" Nova presses her lips together. "Shouldn't we wait for the others to get back?"

"Nah," I say casually, grinning at her. "I'm all amped up. Best do it while I'm in the mood."

Nova watches me climb out of bed. Slightly hesitantly, she gets up too, and takes fresh clothes from the bag.

I pull the shutters closed, so the room descends back into darkness.

"Okay," I tell her. "Let's do this."

23

NOVA

In the dim light of the bedroom, Tanner kneels on the floor. He's shirtless, in just his white boxers. When he looks up at me, his eyes swim with something I haven't seen before. I stroke his face. He leans against my stomach. Then he squeezes my hand and says, "Pass me something to use as a blindfold."

I take a scarf from the bag—Rev clearly pictures us being here until the colder weather sets in—and hand it to him.

Tanner wraps the dark blue scarf tightly around his face, obscuring his eyes. "Usually," he says, sitting down cross-legged, "I tether myself with water. But I think this time I'll use you."

"Tether?" My throat constricts. Something about this doesn't feel right. "Tanner, I really think we should wait—" He grabs my hand and nudges me to sit in front of him.

"We'll do it now," he says darkly. "We'll do it now."

As he begins to mutter, the air shivers. His hand is on my leg. He squeezes hard and mutters something I don't understand. It's the same language we used to cast the masking spell, but what he's saying feels darker. More dangerous.

My skin prickles before ice-cold air grips my bones. Tanner's head snaps back, his face raised toward the ceiling.

He's still muttering. His body shakes. Then he is absolutely still.

When he comes around, he's clasping at the blindfold, throwing it to the ground, and panting as he falls into me and rests his head on my chest. He holds me tight but doesn't speak.

I hear the others downstairs. *Kole… Tanner needs you!* I reach out, searching for Kole's voice.

Seconds later, his heavy feet are on the stairs. He enters and comes straight to us. Kneeling at my elbow, he spots the blindfold and grits his teeth. Jaw clenched, he turns Tanner's face toward him. "Did you jump? Tanner? Did you jump again?"

Tanner opens his eyes. Fear tugs at my belly. Whatever Tanner just did, it has hurt him. I can see it etched on his face. Tanner's lips move, but I can't understand what he's saying. I lower my ear to his mouth. "I found him. He's at *Spine*."

Then Tanner passes out.

We are crowded around the bed, waiting for Tanner to wake. Luther has positioned himself between me and Kole, and he looks pissed.

"First, you let Kole taste your blood to unlock your memories. Now, you're making Tanner jump so we can find your brother?" His eyes dance with fire.

"I didn't…" I push my hands through my hair. "He didn't tell me it was dangerous."

"Didn't you notice the way he's been since we pulled you and Kole out of the hotel?" Luther squares up to me. "On edge? Headaches he can't shift?"

I open my mouth to speak but no sound comes out. In all that's been happening, I didn't even think to ask Tanner how he found us. Guilt washes over me. Mack puts a firm hand on my shoulder and glowers at Luther. "Enough, Luther. She didn't know."

"Of course, you'll protect her," Luther spits.

"Where's this coming from?" Mack asks calmly. "You believe she's the phoenix, just as we do. So, if risks have to be taken—"

"There's a difference between risk and stupidity. We didn't even discuss it." Luther is simmering, literally. Wisps of smoke plume up from his shoulders.

Tanner's voice interrupts him. "It's not her fault. I didn't explain the process."

I dodge around Luther and go to sit on the bed next to Tanner.

"Sorry, Little Star. Didn't mean to scare you."

I stroke his face. "I'm sorry too. If I'd known it might hurt you—"

"If you'd known, you'd have done it anyway," Luther growls.

"Enough." Kole flashes him an angry stare. "Why don't we focus on what's important?" He folds his arms in front of his chest, his Viking frame suddenly taking up more room. "Nova and I heard the voice and shared a vision. We've been trying to work out what to do next to ensure the prophecy comes to fruition. Well, the voice told us—find the wolf. Find Sam. So, yeah, even if it did hurt Tanner. It needed to be done."

He moves his gaze to Tanner, who nods at him. He knows Kole's not being emotionless; he's saying what needs to be said.

Luther doesn't reply.

"He's at *Spine,*" Tanner says, accepting a glass of water and some small pink painkillers from Mack. He downs them in one gulp.

"*Spine?*" Mack sits on the other side of the bed while Kole and Luther remain standing. "You're sure?"

"What's *Spine?*" I ask, unable to let go of Tanner's clammy hand because I've never seen him shaken before. Not like this.

"A club," Luther replies. "A sex club."

I swallow hard. "Sam's working in a sex club?" I turn back to Tanner. "What did you see?"

"He was dancing." Tanner tilts his head to the side and frowns. "People were in the audience. Doing... all kinds of stuff while they watched."

"Where is this place?" I ask, standing up as if I'm ready to leave right this second.

"Red Rock," Mack replies, "but, Nova, it's not a nice place. A lot of what goes on there is highly illegal. We need to talk about how we approach this."

"Red Rock?" My stomach lurches like I'm at the top of a roller-coaster. "He's in Red Rock? He's been this close the whole time?" I look around at the guys. "So, let's go. Let's get him out."

"We will." Mack fixes me with his steely eyes. "But we need to think it through. Our faces are all over the news."

"I'll go." Luther speaks up. "I know the area. When we investigated the FHB ring in Phoenix Falls, I made contacts on that side of town. There's a place I can stay overnight with very little CCTV. Won't be hard to stay unseen. Plus, *Spine* is pretty much an 'anonymous only' kind of joint."

"I'll come." Tanner tries to sit up but cries out and grips his head. "Maybe not." He sinks back onto the pillows.

"I don't think I should." Kole looks annoyed with himself. "In a couple of days, maybe. Right now, I'm too wired."

I look at Mack, expecting him to volunteer next but, instead, he shakes his head. "No shifters allowed." He sighs. "Luther, can you handle it alone?"

As they start to talk amongst themselves, fire crackles in my belly. "What about me?" I put my hands on my hips. "You're not even considering that I might want to go? That I'd be just as useful as any of you." I raise my eyebrows at them. Mack clears his throat sheepishly.

"Nova, it's not that—"

"It's not fair for Luther to go alone. I'm going too. Anyone feel like stopping me?"

When Luther pulls up in front of a large, expensive-looking house with a neat B&B sign out front, I lean forward in my seat and frown at it. "This doesn't look like the best venue for being undercover. I was expecting somewhere…"

"Seedier? Like a dank motel?" Luther asks, pulling onto a gravel driveway that leads to the back of the property.

I raise my eyebrows, taking in the neat white coving, slate roof, and large windows.

"I know the owners. They're discreet." Luther parks the car and climbs out. From the back, he grabs our overnight bag. "This way."

Walking toward the house, my feet crunch on the gravel. Instead of going to the front door, Luther stops at the back entrance and takes out his cell. He dials a number he seems to know by heart. It rings several times, then someone answers and Luther says, "It's me. I need a room."

He hangs up without waiting for a reply. Moments later, the door opens, and a short, round-stomached mage answers. Older than Luther, even Mack, and barely my height, he looks up at us through thick-rimmed glasses. His eyes look comically large beneath the lenses.

Without speaking, he nods and moves aside to let us in. Down the corridor in front of us, I can see a large winding staircase and a beautiful high-ceilinged entrance hall. A curved visitor's desk displays a sign that says, *Ring for Service*. Behind it, brass keys hang on small hooks behind a glass screen.

But instead of going to the desk, we turn right. A little further down the hall, the man opens a door and ushers us through into a stairwell where a series of steps curve down into darkness.

Instead of showing us the way, the man takes a key from his waistcoat pocket and hands it to Luther. This one is black and shiny. "The usual," he says.

Luther nods.

Then the man turns and leaves us.

"Ladies first." Luther steps back and gestures for me to take the stairs down. I wait for a light to come on and illuminate the stairs. When it doesn't, I snap a flame into my palm and use that instead.

"You're getting better," Luther says quietly. "More control."

"With small things, yes," I tell him. "Big things… when I'm fired-up." I pause and shake my head at myself. "No pun intended."

"You mean you lose control when emotion takes over?"

"Yes."

We've reached the bottom of the steps. Luther moves around me and follows a similarly dark corridor past a series of doors with no numbers or handles. "It's harder for fire mages. Our emotions live closer to the surface. We run hot." He glances at me. "In more ways than one."

I'm trying to figure out whether Luther just flirted with me or if I completely misinterpreted what he said when he stops and points at a door. It looks no different from any of the others.

Luther takes the key and, holding it in his hand, whispers, "*Uvam kur ka, e roqa sra daae.*"

A keyhole appears. He slots the key into it and turns, this time muttering, "*Lisrar Rukk.*" He repeats the incantation until the door clunks and swings open.

I hold my breath and follow him inside.

"This is it?" I ask, staring at the room. "This is the top-secret room?"

Luther throws our bag onto the bed. Just one bed, I've noticed. "What were you hoping for? A waterbed and a fancy bathtub?"

I walk across the room in just a few paces. It's tiny and contains nothing but a small double bed, a minibar, and a dark wooden desk. A door to the right of the bed opens onto an ensuite with one sink, a toilet, and a shower. "I just thought—top-secret hotel, fancy magick key." I shrug and sit down on the end of the bed. "I thought it would be less... basic."

"Basic is kind of the point." Luther skims his hand over the desk. "People who use these rooms want security, privacy, and anonymity. They're not so interested in creature comforts."

"Right." I cross one leg over the other and cock my head. "And you've used this place before?"

Luther's eyes narrow.

"Your friend said *the usual*."

He doesn't reply, just takes out his phone and turns it to me. Pointing at the map on the screen, he says, "The club is here. We're here. It opens at midnight."

"It *opens* at midnight?" A yawn scratches at my throat just thinking about having to stay up that late.

"If you're tired, you can sleep while I go fetch some supplies."

"Supplies?" I un-cross and re-cross my legs.

Luther stands back as his gaze trails down my body. It warms my skin and makes me shuffle uncomfortably. He's still mad at me —has been since I arrived in town—but now and then something else flickers in his face. Whatever it is makes me more uncomfortable than his anger.

"Nova, your brother works in a supernatural fetish club. It's not a jeans and tank tops kind of place."

Color rushes to my cheeks. "So, you're going outfit shopping? For both of us?"

"The less you're out and about, the better." Luther shoves his wallet into his back pocket. "I won't be long."

He's at the door when my embarrassment fades and I call to him, "Wait…"

Luther's shoulders ripple; he's sighing at me. "Yes?"

"How will you know what size to buy?"

He turns around, presses his lips together, then rubs the back of his neck. "I'll guess."

I stand up and put my hands on my hips. "That's a terrible idea."

"Nova, we're not picking out a prom dress. We just need to fit in."

"*Okaaay.*" I squeeze past the bed. "But men usually suck at guessing a woman's bra size. And if you get it wrong, I quite literally won't *fit in.*"

A hint of a smile curls the corner of his mouth, but he bites his lower lip to get rid of it. "So, tell me your size."

I'm about to answer when I have a better idea. I grab the bag and rifle through it. "Here." I take out the spare bra and panties Rev sent me and offer them to him.

"Sizing can vary. I'm guessing this naughty clothes store you're going to will have a sales assistant who knows what they're doing. Give them these."

Luther is staring at me as if I'm trying to pass him illegal drugs or a venomous snake. "Right." He takes them quickly and bundles them into his jacket pocket. "Fine." He turns back to the door. "See you."

Then he's gone.

24

LUTHER

I walk the two blocks from Merv's hotel to *Periapt*—a store I've heard lots about but never had the cause to frequent.

With each step, the knowledge that I've got Nova's underwear in my pocket sends an uncomfortable shiver through me. Not arousal, but something close to it. Probably guilt; Nova's my brothers' girl, and I've got her panties in my pocket. Not only that, I'm about to visit a fucking fetish club with their girl. Hell, I'm on my way to pick out the sluttiest outfit I can find and dress her up in it. All while Mack nurses an injured leg, Tanner fights his crippling headaches, and Kole tries to stop ripping up the forest.

How's that right? How have *I* ended up being the one to do this?

Tanner's words as we left the cabin ring in my ears: *At least Luther won't get distracted. He's above all that.*

Right. I'm above all that... I click my tongue loudly. I might not like the girl, but do they seriously think I haven't noticed she's hot as hell? The literal definition of fire.

Especially the last few days, waltzing around the cabin—*my* cabin—wearing barely anything. Fucking Tanner and Kole while she wears *my* t-shirt. The sounds of her orgasms bleeding down through the ceiling while I sit in the living room and try to fight the erection straining in my pants.

I shake my head and try to forget the fact I'm going to be sharing a room with her tonight. After, of course, an evening together at *Spine*—the filthiest club in the state.

Finally, I'm at the store. I push the door open, and a bell rings. With the Bureau hunting us down, it's a terrible time to be out in public. But these kinds of places are designed to be discreet.

Inside, I'm greeted by row upon row of items I can't interpret. Toys, implements, and hangers with what looks like nothing more than leather straps hanging from them.

I stop in front of a mannequin. It has strange, pointed, plastic boobs and a too-tiny waist. But the outfit could work. I'm searching for an assistant when someone lightly touches my shoulder. A guy about Tanner's age with long blond hair, dark makeup around his eyes, and piercings along his top lip.

"Can I help you, Sir?" he asks, eyes widening as he looks from me to the mannequin. "For you? Or a friend?"

Trying to seem like the kind of guy who does this all the time, I smile casually and take Nova's underwear from my pocket. "I'm looking for something for my girlfriend. A surprise. Do you have this in her size?"

The blond guy lifts Nova's bra and panties, examines the labels, then smiles at me. "I surely do. I'll be right back." He returns her clothes to me and disappears out back.

While he's gone, my eyes travel the shelves behind the counter. An array of vibrators, rings, and plugs.

"Here we go…" The blond guy returns and hands me a complicated ensemble that I guess, when put together, will mirror the outfit on the mannequin.

"Great. Thank you. I'll take it."

"And for yourself?" He folds his arms and looks me up and down.

"Me?"

The guy lowers his voice. "Most first-timers who come in here are in town for the same reason." He raises an arched eyebrow. "Tickets to *Spine*?"

Clearly, he's not buying for a second that I do this all the time, so I go with it and shrug a little. "You got me."

"Well, then it's not just your girl who'll need to dress up." The blond guy strokes his chin and looks me up and down. "We need to fix you up, too." He bites his lower lip, then says, "Do you trust me?"

"I don't trust anyone," I reply.

"Sensible," the guy says. "But in this instance, I can assure you that you're in safe hands."

It's nearly dark when I return to Merv's place where I find Nova sleeping. She doesn't wake when I walk in. Her phone is next to her, screen unlocked. I glance at it and see Tanner's name. Tilting my head, I scan the message for anything important.

Tanner: *I'm okay, Little Star. Don't worry about me.*

Nova: *Will you explain it to me when I get back? The jumping? How it works? I feel like there's this huge part of you I don't' understand.*

Tanner: *I promise. Now, go find your brother.*

Tanner: *Just don't have too much fun tonight.*

Nova: *With Luther? Chance would be a fine thing.*

Tanner: *Well, when all this is over, how about you and I head back to Spine for a date night?*

Nova: *Only if Kole and Daddy come too.*

Tanner: *Deal.*

I step back from the bed and bite down a growl of annoyance. Daddy? Mack is into that shit? I dump the bag hard on the end of the bed. The movement jolts her awake, but when she sees me, she smiles.

"Luther, you're back." She searches for a window to check whether it's light out, remembers there isn't one, then says, "What's the time?"

"Late. Time to eat." Next to the bag, I set down a large takeout pizza. Nova opens the box and grabs a slice without hesitation.

I linger for a moment, standing, then she pats the bed for me to sit down. She sits up, cross-legged, and nudges the box in my direction. Looking at the bag, she asks, "Successful trip?"

"I think so."

"Should I be scared?" she smiles cheekily at me.

"Depends how much you like leather," I reply, biting into my slice and letting the molten cheese scald my tongue.

Nova pauses, pizza halfway to her mouth.

"You don't like it?" I ask, frowning.

"No, I do. It's just…" She flattens her hand on her stomach. "Not sure I should eat a tray full of carbs before squeezing into something *fetishy*."

"Don't be ridiculous." I jerk my head at the pizza. "You'll be fine. Eat up."

"Wow." She rolls her eyes and mutters, "You sure know how to flatter a girl."

I open my mouth to reply but decide there's no good way to answer her. Instead, I hand her a bottle of beer from the minibar and flick the cap off with my thumb.

"Thanks." She takes it from me and swigs down a large mouthful. I catch myself watching her throat as she swallows. Get a hold of yourself, Luther. Now is not the time.

"No problem."

We finish the rest of the pizza in silence. Nova is texting—Kole this time—while I check for information about *Spine*; dress code, etiquette, rules. Finally, it's time to get ready.

"You can change in the bathroom. I'll wait out here." I take my outfit from the bag, then hand the rest of the contents to Nova.

"You have something too?" She tilts her head, trying to make out what I'm holding.

"'Fraid so." My jaw twitches.

"Okay, well that makes me feel better." She smiles nervously. Would she be nervous if she was dressing up for Tanner, or Kole, or Mack? Probably not.

"You'll be fine," I say for the second time this evening. "Shout if you need help."

Nova's forehead creases, as if she's not sure what on earth she could need my help with, but then she disappears into the bathroom and locks the door behind her.

She's in there for what seems like forever. Finally, the door clicks. But when it opens, only Nova's head sticks out. "Hand me my coat," she says. I look round the room. Her long brown coat is in our overnight bag. I take it out and put it into her hand. There's a shuffling sound. Her head disappears, then she's back. All I can see of the outfit I chose is the pair of black knee-high boots sticking out from the bottom of the coat.

When she catches me staring, she shrugs and says, "You don't need to see it now, do you?"

Slightly awkwardly, aware a slow heat is creeping down my back, I stand up. "No. I mean, if it fits and you're okay with it?"

"It fits." She wraps her arms around her waist. "I'll get into character when we get there." She looks at the mini bar under the desk. "I just might need a few more drinks first."

25

NOVA

I expected to be exhausted by midnight, but the adrenaline prickling in my veins is keeping me wide awake. Thinking of seeing Sam makes my head spin. I feel completely unprepared, like this is all happening far too quickly. At the same time, though, deep inside I know it *has* to happen like this.

We walk to the club. It feels risky to be out in the open like this, but Luther's adamant this is the last place the Bureau would look for us. Besides, he says, this part of town is light on CCTV. An unwritten rule, because the city fat cats want it to stay that way, which says these streets should remain a place of darkness and anonymity.

The boots Luther bought me are already hurting my heels, but the way they click against the sidewalk makes me feel somehow more confident. Like a risqué catwalk model. Although, that could be from the beer and the two large whiskey and cokes I had before we left.

I have no idea how I'm going to feel when I actually have to take my coat off. I've never worn an outfit like this in my life; part of me feels like Luther must have asked for the *least* amount of clothing possible just to tease me. And the panties? I almost refused to wear them when I noticed they had no crotch. But now, to my surprise, I'm realizing that the sensation of cool night air between my legs is more than a little pleasant. Maybe I'll take them home when we're done. I'd *love* to see Mack's face if I bent over his desk wearing these.

"Nova?" Luther gestures for me to walk faster. I still haven't seen all of his outfit. Like me, he changed in the bathroom and pulled his jacket on top. I have, however, seen his leather pants. At first, they made me giggle, but now I can't help wondering what's on his top half.

Before we left, I told him to sit down on the bed and smudged dark makeup around his eyes to match what I'd done to my own. It suits him. Emphasizes his stupidly long eyelashes and the tone of his skin.

The club, of course, is situated down a narrow alleyway. At the back, people file quietly toward a large metal door. They're asked questions by a thick-necked pair of mages, then show the tickets on their phones, and are allowed past.

"What are they asking?" I whisper to Luther.

"No idea." He puts his hand on the small of my back. "Let me do the talking."

At the front of the queue, the mage on the left looks casually at Luther and says, "Been here before?"

I expect Luther to say yes, but he shakes his head and makes a show of squeezing his arm around my waist. His eyes sparkle a little as he says, "No, it's our first time."

"You read the rules?"

Luther nods.

"Tickets?"

Luther shows his phone.

"Fire mage and fire witch." The bouncer nods. "Fire play is on the third floor. Enjoy." He stands to one side. The door clunks open.

We're in an elevator. It is pitch black and silent, but I can feel it taking us down below ground level. When it stops, the doors slide open. Instantly, a heavy beat fills my ears and vibrates down through my body. We emerge in a corridor thick with people. I feel hands on my shoulders and spin around to see a man with a bare chest and pierced nipples taking my jacket.

Luther nods at me as he shrugs out of his own jacket and hands it over. My eyes widen. He's wearing an asymmetric black shirt, cap-sleeve on one side, tank top on the other. Down its center, a ladder of slashed fabric shows snatches of his dark skin and toned torso.

It hugs his frame in all the right places, and he doesn't seem a bit self-conscious as he thanks the jacket-taking guy. Wishing I had another whiskey, I straighten my shoulders and imagine that, instead of being surrounded by people, I'm standing in front of Mack's mirror. Kole behind me. *Do you see what I see?*

When I open my eyes, Luther is staring at me.

"Is it okay?" I whisper.

He nods. "Good." His eyes skim from my waist, cinched in by a tight black corset that finishes just above my hips, to my breasts. The corset is molded into half-cups, only just covering my nipples, pushing my chest into impressive peaks.

Stretching from the sides of my breasts, thick black straps loop up and join another that's fastened around my neck like a collar. The collar is attached to another strap that hangs down to meet the top of my suspenders. The suspender belt presses tight against my skin, thick in the middle, but fanning out in cords that smooth over my hips and ass.

"Really… fine." Luther swallows hard, then quickly adds, "You wear it better than the mannequin."

I tilt my head at him. "Is that a compliment?"

Luther doesn't reply, just takes my hand. He is hot to the touch. "Tanner talked about a stage with people watching. Look for something that matches his description."

As we move down the corridor, the thud of the music grows louder. It reverberates through my bones, sending shivers up my arms. If I thought my outfit was revealing, there are people wearing far more daring and elaborate ensembles. But Luther, to my surprise, doesn't let his gaze linger.

I'm finding it more difficult to stay focused. For so long, all I knew was Johnny. Stiff, rigid, joyless sex. Since I arrived in Phoenix Falls, it's like I've been slowly awakening. Learning it's possible to feel so many things in so many ways.

We pass a room with a large open door. My eyes catch on flashes of flesh. Bodies. Lots of bodies, whose collective groans make my pussy throb; something about this place is intoxicating. The smells, the sounds, the magick that hangs in the air.

"Keep moving." Luther tugs my hand.

I follow him, trying to focus on the reason we're here, but unable to not notice the things that are happening around us. As we cross through a bar, a mage stands in the center of the room. A woman, a water witch like Tanner, is on her knees in front of him. Instead of touching him, she's moving an envelope of swirling water up and down his large erection using just flicks of her hands.

When he comes, his semen merges with the water, making it paler. The water witch tips her head back and drinks it down, smiling as it splashes her throat and her naked breasts.

"Nova." Luther stops and meets my eyes. "You okay?"

I nod. My mouth is dry. "Fine."

He cocks his head to the side. His fingers twitch as if he's thinking of running them over the black strap down my middle. Then he says, "Okay, then let's keep moving."

On a lit-up screen at the end of the bar, Luther finds a list of rooms and levels. He taps it and turns to me. "Wolf Dance. Room Five. Bingo."

I realize I'm squeezing his hand tightly and release my grip. As we pass the bar, he stops and gets us each a shot of something bright green and revolting. I swallow it down fast. It burns my throat and brings tears to my eyes but helps drown out the nerves in my stomach.

Moving down to the next floor, the lighting becomes darker and the music louder. A hand brushes my hip. Not Luther's. Another tugs on the black cord around my neck. Luther notices and wraps a fierce arm around me. Fire prickles on his shoulders. Flames lick his skin. He allows them to grow until a security guard shouts, "Fire in the fire-play rooms only."

Luther raises an apologetic hand and cools the flames but when we start moving again, he walks beside me like a sentinel. Tall, protective.

Room Five is behind a closed red door. Luther pushes it open and ushers me through. Inside, I blink and try to focus. The room is almost pitch dark, but as my eyes adjust, I realize there are rows of small, high-backed couches, arranged in a semi-circle around a dark stage.

I point at it. Luther nods.

Hand on the small of my back, he guides me through the rows. I expect to see people fucking in the darkness but they're all sitting, waiting, watching the empty stage.

When we find a vacant couch, Luther sits down and pats the seat next to him. I haven't practiced sitting in this contraption, and the feeling of warm leather beneath my crotch makes me flinch. I turn to Luther. He's staring at me but looks away quickly.

"See something you like?" I whisper playfully, trying to lighten the tense, quivering atmosphere between us.

Luther leans forward onto his knees. "The boys are very lucky," he says quietly.

Before he can say anything else, a low vibration, like drums beneath the floor, spreads through the room. It makes my feet tingle in my boots. Luther sits up.

There's another vibration, louder this time, then spotlights rain down on the stage, illuminating a single shining pole.

Music begins to play. There's no melody or tune, just waves of notes that send shivers from my head to my toes.

A figure appears on stage. A black mask shields the top half of

his face. The bottom displays a square jaw and a dusting of stub-
ble. On one side of his torso, an armored shield stretches from
his shoulder down his arm. His legs are clad in dark leather, a
silver buckle shining on his belt.

The crowd is silent.

The man turns to face the pole, puts his hands on it, then levers
himself up. He starts to move to the music, and I'm transfixed.
His muscles undulate with each flip and turn. He's upside down,
then the right way up. His legs open wide, his hips chime a
rhythm that makes my heart race. And the shapes he makes with
his body…

Luther's hand on my thigh makes me jump. He tweaks his finger
under my chin and turns my head, so I scan the room. On every
single couch, couples are starting to play with each other. Not
fucking. Not yet, and not just couples. Threesomes. Groups.
More bodies than I can count.

"This guy must be the warm-up act," Luther whispers. Then he
nudges my elbow. "Sit on my lap."

I frown at him. He tugs me on top of him, my ass landing hard
on his crotch. "The guard by the door is staring at us," he says,
running his hands over my arms. "We're supposed to be
enjoying ourselves. If we look like undercover cops, we'll be
tossed out. And we won't be getting back in."

I reach back and pull his mouth closer to my neck.

"Is he Sam?" Luther asks, so close that I feel his breath on my
skin.

"I don't know. He could be." I look up at the stage, wriggling my hips so it looks like I'm enjoying the way Luther is nuzzling me.

A small grunt parts his mouth. He shifts beneath me. "Easy," he says. "We're pretending, remember?"

Across the room, the security guard has left his post and is now weaving in and out of the crowd. Shit. He's coming toward us.

Spinning around, straddling Luther, I bend down and whisper, "Did *you* remember that we're pretending when you picked this outfit?"

Luther's hands rest lightly on my waist. His fingers twitch on my skin. "It was the first one I saw."

Watching the security guard pace along the row behind us, his eyes darting over to us as he moves, I sit up. Luther's eye-level with my breasts.

Hooking my thumb in the waistband of my panties, I tweak my hips a little. "Did you know these were crotchless when you bought them?"

Luther's mouth drops open. He looks down at my thighs. "Are you serious?" he hisses.

"Yes. I'm serious. Are you telling me you didn't know?"

The guard is directly behind our couch now. He meets my eyes. Then I realize he has his dick in his hand. He smirks at me and looks purposefully down at it. He edges closer, but I quickly turn around and slide my back down Luther's chest, slamming his hands onto my tits.

"Nova? What the—"

"He's not suspicious of us," I snarl. "He's just a horny asshole who's hoping to get in on the action."

Luther glances over his shoulder, then chuckles. Realizing his hands are still on my corseted breasts, he shifts them to my hips instead.

On stage, the dancer is reaching the climax of his performance. The music crescendos. The vibrations intensify. Then the lights go out.

When they come on again, a chain is hanging from the pole with a leather collar attached to the end of it.

The dancer steps around the front of the pole, kneels, and locks the collar around his neck. As he snaps it shut, and his wrist turns, I grab Luther's hand. "There. Can you see it? The birth-mark." I squeeze his fingers with mine. "It's him, Luther, we found him."

But the jittery excitement in my chest soon fades. On stage, Sam turns his back to the audience and begins to remove his clothes.

"What are those marks?" I ask Luther, leaning forward in his lap. "I thought they were tattoos but they look more like—"

I hear a small intake of breath. "Fighting scars."

"Fighting?"

"Nova." He clutches my waist. "I don't think you want to stay for this. We've found him. We know he's here. We'll come back tomorrow and—"

"Are you kidding? I'm not leaving." I try to move off his knees, but Luther keeps me pinned in place.

"Nova. What's about to happen... I've heard about it. It's not—"

His words are cut off by a howl. A gut-wrenching, wall-shaking, howl. When I look back at the stage, Sam is standing stock-still. And a pack of wolves has surrounded him.

26

SAM

As the spotlights heat up, and the other wolves file onto the stage, my eyes land on a girl. She has long silver hair, and eyes that make me want to never look into another woman's eyes ever again.

Two different colors. One blue, one brown.

They remind me of my sister.

I shake my head to dislodge the image. The movement rattles the chain. The other wolves snap and snarl, interpreting it as a sign I'm ready to start.

As they come for me, one by one, I fix my gaze on her. She's with a guy. Big, rippling muscles. A fire mage, if I had to guess, because he gives off a 'fuck with me and I'll burn you' vibe that I've seen many times before.

Now and then, she shifts in his lap, but they're not fucking. They're the only couple in the room not fucking.

I'm on the floor, teeth sinking into my shoulder, when she runs forward.

27

NOVA

For ten long minutes, we watch a pack of wolves slash at my brother with their teeth and their claws. They're not trying to kill him—that much is obvious—but I don't understand what's happening.

All around us, people are groaning, yelping with pleasure as they watch his skin break and bleed.

"He's a werewolf. Why doesn't he shift and fight them off?" I ask Luther.

Once again, he tries to make me leave. "Nova, let's talk outside." But I refuse because Sam is watching me.

His eyes locked onto me when the wolves started howling, and they haven't left me since. He knows who I am. I can feel it.

"Nova, please." Luther squeezes my hand. "We can come back tomorrow."

Until now, Sam has managed to stay standing, but now he sinks to all fours. A wolf rips the armored sleeve from his arm. Another plunges its teeth into his shoulder. A third leaps on his back and drags its claws down his skin. Sam cries out. A woman nearby claps and cheers as blood pools on the stage.

I jump from Luther's grasp and rush forward. "Get away from him!" I leap onto the stage, waving my arms and then curling myself over his body. People shout and jeer. The wolves back off, snarling, eyes darting, unsure what to do.

The security guard yells at me to get the fuck down.

"Sam, it's me. It's Nova."

Through his black leather mask, his eyes meet mine. "Nova?"

"I'm going to get you out of here. I'm going to take you home." I reach for the mask, desperate to free his face.

"I can't leave," he whispers. "They won't let me."

There are hands are on my waist. I hear Luther yell, "Get the fuck off her!" but the hands are pulling me away.

"I'll be back," I shout.

Sam closes his eyes.

"I'll be back!" I shout again, but the security guard throws me to the floor.

"No, you fucking won't." He towers above me, looking like he's going to kick me with his huge bulky boots.

Luther steps in front of him. Flames are in his hands. "If you touch her, I *will* kill you," he growls.

"Then get her the hell out of here before I set them loose." The guard jerks his thumb toward the wolves on stage.

Luther helps me to my feet and wraps his arm around my waist, holding me tight. Saying nothing, he hurries me out of the room.

At the door, another guard meets us and marches us to the elevator. He stands and waits while Luther retrieves our jackets, then accompanies us all the way up and out of the building.

"These two are barred," he says to the guy out front. "For life."

Then the door slams, and we're out in the cold.

We don't speak until we're back at the hotel. Luther unlocks the door and ushers me inside. He sits down hard on the edge of the bed and rubs his hands over his closely shaved hair.

"Shit, Nova."

"I'm sorry." I'm standing in front of the bathroom door. It's closed, and I'm leaning against it. My heart is still thundering in my chest. "I just don't understand what they were doing."

"It's fucked up," Luther says darkly. "And illegal, which is the only reason they didn't call the cops on you."

I bite my lower lip. "People get off on that? Why? How?"

Luther inhales slowly. He's pissed at me, but he bites his tongue. "What's important is that we found him. We found Sam." Luther glances at me. "What did he say to you? Did he recognize you?"

"I think so, but he said he can't leave. '*They* won't let me leave.' Those were his words." I shake my head and sink down onto the floor, coat still wrapped around my too-exposed body. "What the hell did he get himself into? How did he end up in that place?"

Luther moves and sits beside me. He puts his hand on mine. "We found him," he says firmly, as if all that other stuff doesn't matter. "Now we just have to figure out a way to get him out."

28

LUTHER

Nova emerges from the bathroom in a long white tee. Kole's, if I had to guess. Her hair is wet. She spent a long time under the hot water and still looks like a deer in head-lights. Like everything she saw and felt in there is too much to process.

I hand her a mug of tea. "Here."

It's four a.m.. We should sleep, but we're both too wired.

"Thank you." She takes the mug, sits down, and rests her back on the pillows, drawing her knees up underneath her.

For a moment, I linger by the desk.

"Are you going to change, or do you think you'll stick with the new look?" she asks, eyeing my leather pants.

I look down at them, almost certain I can see a shadow from where she pressed herself into me in those barely-there panties. I clear my throat as my dick twitches, put down my tea, jerk off the pants and the shirt, then shrug and say, "There. Back to normal."

Nova looks at me over the rim of her mug but says nothing. Shifting over a little, she says, "Looks like we're sharing?"

"Looks like it." I move next to her and perch on the side of the bed. "I can sleep in the car if you'd rather?"

"That doesn't sound very safe." She puts her mug down on the nightstand, then tucks her legs beneath the sheets.

"You're tired?" I ask, glancing at her.

"My head's throbbing," she says. "Not sure if it's from exhaustion or emotion." She trails off and reaches back to loosely braid her hair. She hasn't removed her eye makeup. It emphasizes the difference between the blue and the brown of her eyes. "Seeing him like that. Letting them do those things to him. The dancing I get, but the fighting?" She looks at me and adds, "I'm not judging him."

I look away and down my last mouthful of tea. "Of course not."

The club was such a mind-fuck that, until it all kicked off with the wolves, I almost forgot we were there on business. Since we left, all that's been pulsing through my brain has been Nova. The feel of her. The smell of her. The *sight* of her in that outfit.

"Have you figured it out yet?" she asks, staring at me.

"Huh?" I need to get my head back in the game.

"How we'll get him out? You said you'd come up with a plan."

I swing my legs up and slide under the covers. Nova lies down on her side, facing me. Once again, the knowledge I'm in bed with my brothers' girl makes me shift uncomfortably.

"I think so." I'm on my back but look at her sideways. "Sam said they won't *let* him leave—if he's indentured to the club, it means whoever owns the place bought him. They paid for him. He's their property. So, there's pretty much only one thing that could secure his release."

Nova sits up on her elbow.

"Money," I tell her. "If we offer the owner enough money, he *might* let Sam go."

"You're saying we have to buy him? We buy my brother?"

I lace my fingers together behind my head, jutting out my elbows. "Yes, Nova. We buy your brother." I look at her and add, "It actually kind of works. After what happened… we tell them you saw Sam up on stage and just couldn't stand seeing him hurt like that. Now you want to take him home and make him all better. I'm your husband. I'll do anything to make you happy. We ask how much they want for him—"

"And that'll work?" she asks, frowning.

I breathe in slowly. "If it doesn't, we can get Snow and Kole to tear the place apart. But, given the circumstances, it's best if we avoid causing a scene." I pause, then add, "Any *more* of a scene, that is."

"Do we have that kind of money? How much does a human being cost?"

"First of all, Sam's a werewolf, not a human," I correct her, a little snappily. "Second of all, *a lot* I'd imagine."

Nova repeats her question. "How will we pay them?"

"Daddy Mack will sort it." I give her a knowing glance. For a moment, she tries to look annoyed, then laughs instead. After the heaviness of the last few hours, it's nice to see her smile. And it's nice to think Mack has that effect on her. After all he's been through, it's time he found some happiness.

Lying back on the pillows, Nova reaches for the light switch. The room plunges into darkness.

I hear her wriggling down into the sheets. I swallow hard, wondering if she's thinking about Mack and the things he does to her. She's probably not. She's probably thinking about her brother and all the awful things she just witnessed. But clearly, that club has put my mind in the gutter.

"Luther?"

"Mmm?" My voice comes out croaky. I try again, "Yeah?"

"Why do you hate humans so much?"

I blink up at the pitch-dark ceiling. "I don't hate humans."

"That's not what I've heard."

I sigh, frustrated, and swipe my hand over my face. "Well, you heard wrong. I don't trust humans, but that's not the same as hating them."

"Why?" Her question hangs in the air between us.

"Why?"

"Why don't you trust them?"

I shake my head and laugh a deep laugh. This isn't a conversation I intended to have tonight. In fact, it's a conversation I rarely intend to have. With anyone. "It's a long story."

Nova doesn't speak. I can hear her breath moving up and down in her chest.

I close my eyes. "Okay, I'll give you the short version... I grew up in a town on the cusp of the anti magick belt. Pretty much all pure-blood supers. A place called Solleville. We kept to ourselves and didn't have too many problems. Until the A.M.A. started up in a village nearby." I grip the bedsheet and twist it between my fingers. "I was sixteen. They invaded in the middle of the night."

Nova holds her breath.

"We were sleeping. They had guns. They slaughtered fifty men, women, and children that day. Went house-by-house, murdering them in their sleep."

"Luther..." she breathes. Her hand finds me and comes to rest on my arm. My muscles tense. As a fire mage, most women I've been with feel cold to the touch. Even witches with a fire affinity rarely run hot enough for me. But when Nova presses her skin to mine, it's like I'm being touched by the sun itself.

I move her hand to my chest. To the small scar next to my heart. I press her finger to it. "They missed by a couple of inches. I survived. My parents did not."

She doesn't take her hand away. My chest rises into her palm as I breathe slowly in and out. Warmth settles in my lungs. "I'm so sorry," she whispers. She's silent for a moment, then I feel like she's going to say something.

Her hand is still on my chest. Her fingers twitch as if they might start stroking me gently. But she doesn't.

"Thank you for telling me," she says quietly.

I don't reply. Emotion is constricting my throat, making it impossible to speak.

After a while, I feel her turn over. A little while after that, her breathing changes. She's asleep.

When I wake, Nova is asleep with her back toward me. The bedsheets are tangled around her legs, her bare ass jutting out from beneath them, her tee ridden up around her waist. My balls are throbbing. I barely slept. Talking about my past is not something I do often, and the only way I could stop from thinking about it was to think about her instead.

The way she looked at the club. The way she *felt* while she was on top of me.

Did you know these were crotchless when you bought them?

The memory of her hot breath on my ear makes me instantly hard.

I roll onto my back and put my hand on my dick. Images of last night dance in front of my eyes. The corset that only half-covered her breasts, nipples dangerously close to being exposed. The straps that wound up from the corset to loop around her neck. The leash that dropped from a small silver ring at her throat and fixed to the top of her suspenders. Her thighs. Her ass. All of it.

I look over at her. I could do it here while she's sleeping; make myself come while I stare at her. But what kind of fucking pervert would that make me? Jerking off next to my brothers' girl while she sleeps.

I climb quietly out of bed, go to the bathroom, close the door, and get into the shower. The water runs cold, but I don't care, and it does little to dampen the heat in my veins.

I wrap my hand around my erection and fist it hard, leaning against the tiles and letting the water stream down my face. I drag my fingers over my piercings, wondering what she'd think if she saw them. The ladder of bars down my shaft.

I picture her lowering herself onto me, seeing her eyes widen as my metal strokes her pulsing walls. I imagine pulling the corset down and taking one perfect pink bud between my teeth, biting just enough to send a jolt of pain down her spine. Then soothing it with my tongue, taking the pain away again.

I imagine her tilting her head back so I can trace a line of fire over her skin.

Did you know these were crotchless when you bought them?

As the water grows warmer, I can almost feel her—hot and wet, easing onto my cock. It doesn't take long for an orgasm to rock through me, but it's not the regular kind. It's like a spark that doesn't fully ignite. Barely even any cum. At least, not as much as usual.

I thump the tiles hard with my fist. I'm still hard, and the sensation of being completely unsatisfied makes my chest tight with frustration.

"Luther?" I feel the door open. A rush of cold air sweeps in.

I turn around but can barely see through the steam that's filling the room.

Nova waves a hand in front of her face. "Are you alright? You've been in here ages."

"I'm fine." I grab a towel and push past her, leaving the water running. "Your turn. Be quick. We have business to take care of."

29

NOVA

This time, we drive to the club. Luther parks up in the now-empty alleyway. He's back in his normal clothes, but I chose to keep the boots on over my jeans, coat on top, and reapplied my dark eye makeup.

"Let me talk," Luther says gruffly as we get out of the car.

"You spoke to Mack about the money?" I ask quietly.

Luther is holding his cellphone. He glances at it and says, "It's all in place. I can transfer it as soon as they agree."

Reminding myself to ask Mack later where exactly all his money comes from, I follow Luther to the door. He knocks loud and hard.

He seems different this morning; last night, when he told me about his family, I thought I'd finally broken a chip off his rock-hard exterior. But this morning he was back to being moody and distant. Although, that could be because I caught him masturbating in the shower; he was in there for far too long and doesn't exactly have the excuse of needing to wash his hair.

After what feels like forever, the door opens. A security guard—who, thankfully, I don't recognize from last night—positions himself in the frame. He almost fills it up; taller than Luther and with shoulders, and a thick neck, like one of those weightlifters you see on TV.

Unfortunately, he recognizes us. "You two are barred. Leave before I call the cops." He moves to shut the door, but Luther puts his foot inside it.

"There was a misunderstanding last night," he says calmly. "We're here to clear it up."

"Move." The guard lifts his palm. It's flickering with electricity.

Luther doesn't fire back, just folds his arms and says, "Let me try this another way… let us inside or we'll send video footage of your illegal stage show straight to the SDB."

The guard's jaw twitches. He swallows hard. "What do you want?"

"We want to talk to the owner." Luther puts his hands casually into his pockets. "We have a business proposition we think he'll be very interested in discussing."

"Wait here." The guard slams the door shut. A moment later, it opens again. He's holding his phone to his ear. "Okay, boss. If you're sure."

He hangs up and jerks his head at Luther. "Boss says to bring you to her office."

"*Her?*" I whisper to Luther as we enter the elevator.

He raises his eyebrows but doesn't respond.

When we reach the corridor, which last night was so full of writhing bodies, Luther takes my hand. This time, we veer left through a small unassuming door, down another corridor, through an archway, then stop.

A pair of large oak doors are in front of us. The security guard stands in front of a retinal scanner that beeps and lets him in.

We emerge in what looks like a bedroom. Huge white bathtub in the corner that reminds me of Mack's, a red velvet chaise lounge, and an enormous four-poster bed. A woman emerges from the door near the bathtub. She's wearing a long silk robe, cream-colored, and has ash blond hair that reaches down to her waist. The robe is open just enough to expose a flash of cleavage.

Luther doesn't let go of my hand.

The guard nods at the woman then steps back outside and closes the doors.

Sitting down on the chaise lounge, the woman crosses one long slim leg over the other, places her hands on her knee, and smiles at us. "How can I help you?"

Frowning at her, Luther doesn't answer, just asks his own question. "Why did you let us in?"

Her smile widens. She tucks her hair behind her ear. "You don't have video footage of the wolf dance." She tilts her head. "You lied, and that intrigues me." She sits back, legs still crossed, and nestles her back into the red velvet. "I do have a busy day ahead, however, so you best be quick."

"Alright." Luther steps forward. "I'm sure you're aware my wife found the show a little… upsetting."

The blond woman's forehead creases ever so slightly as she frowns. "Yes. I watched the security tapes."

"She felt an… affinity with the chained wolf." Luther turns away from the woman and looks at me instead. He meets my eyes and smiles. It sends a shiver down my spine. "I love my wife very much," he says, not looking away from me. It almost feels like more than an act, the way he says it.

"That's very sweet." The woman stands up, this time putting her hands on her hips as if she's growing impatient. "So, what is it you're looking for? An apology?"

Luther moves his hand to my waist and gently pulls me closer to him. "We'd like to buy the wolf." He fixes his gaze on the woman in front of us.

For a long moment, no one moves or speaks. Luther holds his nerve while the blond bites her lower lip. "You'd like to buy one of my wolves?"

"Not *one* of your wolves. That particular wolf. The one in the mask."

The woman exhales slowly and clicks her tongue. Then she claps her hands and says loudly to the air, "Bring me Number Five." When she looks back at us, she says, "Take a seat," and gestures to the chaise. "I'll change and be right back. Then we'll have a talk."

At the door to, I assume a walk-in-wardrobe, she looks back and says, "You can call me Madame, by the way."

When she disappears, I look at Luther, trying to meet his eyes, but he hasn't broken his pose. He's staring straight ahead, arm around my shoulders. My heart is hammering in my chest. A shiver snakes through me. With his free hand, Luther takes mine and gently strokes my palm.

Madame emerges wearing a long red dress, hair hanging loose over her shoulders. She's barefoot but tall, and walks straight to the doors to open them.

On the other side, the guard is waiting. Next to him… Sam.

My body jerks with the desire to get up and run to him, but Luther squeezes my thigh hard and keeps me still. "Nearly there," he whispers. "Hold it together."

Like last night, Sam is wearing black pants and a black mask on his face. The shield on his arm has gone. A long-sleeved gray t-shirt covers his torso. He winces as he walks forward.

"Madame," he greets her, lowering his head.

She strokes his chin. "Good morning, Number Five," she says, lowering her lips to his ear. "Did you sleep well?"

"Yes, Madame," he replies, staring straight ahead.

Waving her hand at the guard to tell him to leave, Madame puts her hand on Sam's arm and walks him to the center of the room. "This is the wolf you like?" she asks me.

At that moment, Sam's eyes finally flicker in my direction. They widen, almost imperceptibly, but nothing about his posture changes. He is stock still, hands behind his back, legs apart, waiting.

I look at Luther, then at Sam. "Yes, he's the one."

"And you'd like to buy him?" she looks from me to Luther.

"Yes." Luther stands up and strides forward, ignoring Sam and speaking only to Madame. "How much would you ask for him?"

Twitching her nose, Madame walks a slow circle around Sam's back. She smooths her hands over his shoulders. His breath catches in his chest, but he remains motionless.

She sighs heavily. "If it was any other wolf..." She shakes her head. "You see, Sam is very special. It's rare to find a wolf of his talents." She stops next to him and runs a finger down his side.

"He's an exceptional dancer. Very handsome. Very *strong*." She snaps her eyes toward me. "And a virgin."

I blink several times.

"Sam has been with me since he was sixteen years old. He has never been with a woman, or a man," she laughs, "or a demon." She cups his face with her hand. "He's completely pure." Then she looks at Luther. "Do you know how much he could fetch at auction?"

Nausea and fire swirl in my stomach. I close my eyes and picture Luther's cool breeze soothing my body.

"How much?" Luther asks tightly, handing her his phone with the screen unlocked and the calculator open.

Madame's lips tweak into a smile. She bites her lip, then types in a number and returns the screen to Luther.

"Fine." He doesn't even try to haggle. "I can have it transferred within the hour."

Madame's eyes widen. "Well, well, well. Don't I feel silly? I should have asked for more." She looks at Sam and leans in, dragging her tongue across his jaw. I close my eyes. "Samuel? Would you like to go with these nice people?"

Sam clears his throat. "I will do as you say, Madame."

She hesitates, still close to his face. Then claps her hands again and smiles. "Very well. He's yours. Have the money transferred, and you can come back to collect him at midday."

"We'll take him now." Luther swipes at his phone. "I'll make the transfer now. We leave with him now."

"Oh, come now, Mr...." She frowns, realizing she hasn't asked our names, but then shrugs, rolls her eyes then says, "Fine." She waves at the phone then rattles off an account number. "Do it."

Luther's thumbs move quickly over the screen. He presses a button, answers a call, says, "Yes. I'm authorizing it. Code 3-0-7-1," then hangs up and shows her the confirmation. "Done."

She claps twice. The guard reappears. "My cellphone?" she asks.

He goes to the drawer beside the bed and takes it out. When he hands it to her, she unlocks the screen, then nods slowly. "Very good." She smiles at Sam. "I'm sad to lose you, Samuel. If you ever want to come back, you know where to find us."

Luther takes Sam roughly by the arm. It makes me flinch, but I stand up slowly and take his other arm too.

At the door, Luther pauses and says, "You got a good deal here, Madame. You can buy three new wolves with that money."

She flashes him a pearly smile. "Oh, I know. Do you think I'd have let him go otherwise?"

Outside, Luther opens the back passenger door and gestures for Sam to climb in. I slide into the seat next to him.

"Say nothing until we're out of here," Luther orders, revving the engine.

Just outside town, he pulls over to the side of the road and checks the car for bugs, traces, or tracking spells. When he gets back in, he says, "Okay. All clear."

Immediately, Sam reaches for the mask. He pulls at it, his chest heaving, muscles shaking. He clasps the back, tugging to get it off.

"Here, here, it's okay." I unfasten it for him and ease it off his face. He lets out a small groan, then rubs his hands over his curly dark hair. His shoulders drop. He's looking at the window instead of at me.

"Sam?" I put my hand on him. He lets out a short sharp breath as if my touch hurts him.

"Nova?" His voice is low and unsure. "Am I dreaming all this?"

I catch Luther watching us from the driver's seat as he speeds up and joins the highway. Inching sideways, I place my palm on the side of Sam's face and turn him toward me. "It's me." I meet his eyes. A rush of warmth spreads through me. I take hold of his hand and stroke the mark on his wrist.

"You're alive?" he asks, his breath catching.

"Yes."

"And you found me?"

"Yes."

He stares at me. Tracing his fingers down the sides of my fac, he picks up a strand of hair and frowns at it.

"Long story." I smile.

"It's you." He pulls me to him and holds me close. "It's really you."

30

MACK

The last twenty-four hours have been some of the most painful of my life. After searching for information on Ragnor, and coming up totally blank, all I had left to do was worry about Nova. And try not to think about her being in a sex club with Luther.

The others feel it too. The worry. Tanner's headaches have gone, but he's climbing the walls for news. Kole is in danger of growing an entire rainforest outside, his powers still in overdrive, and Snow is so on edge I can hardly contain him.

When Luther said they'd found Sam and needed money, relief washed through me. "Pay whatever they want," I told him. "Anything to keep Nova out of danger. We don't want to have to physically break him out of there unless we have to."

By the time they arrive, the three of us are waiting outside. "Sounds like it was pretty fucked up," Tanner says darkly. "What they were doing to him in that place."

"You knew that," Kole says. "Didn't you?"

Tanner closes his eyes. "I felt it. I didn't want to scare her."

Kole nods, understanding, and folds his arms. When the car pulls up, Luther is the first to climb out. Tanner's about to rush forward when he says, "They're sleeping in the back. But she's okay. They're both okay."

"What happened?" Kole asks, rubbing his arms as if he's trying to physically restrain himself from going to the car.

"Wolf fights." Luther rubs the back of his neck. "Sam was the victim."

"Shit." I clench my fists.

"Nova watched it. I tried to make her leave…" Luther trails off. I've rarely seen him like this; he has a haunted look on his face. "The whole place was a head-fuck," he says darkly.

"Hey…" Nova's voice makes us all look round. She's stepped out of the car. My eyes snap to her legs. Knee-high boots with a heel. Her coat is hanging open. She runs to Tanner. He wraps his arms around her waist, beneath the coat. Kole kisses her neck. I hold back, but when Snow growls at me, I slip my hand into hers. Letting Tanner go, Nova folds herself under my chin. "Thank you." She reaches up and kisses me. "Thank you for getting him out."

Luther clears his throat loudly, making Nova turn around. Sam is unfolding himself gingerly from the back passenger seat. He blinks into the daylight. Dark, slightly curly hair, over six-feet tall, a lithe but toned frame hidden beneath a plain gray tee and a pair of black leather pants.

"Guys," Nova says, taking Sam's hand. "This is Sam." She rubs his arm with her other hand. "Sam, this is everyone. Kole, Tanner, Mack, and…" she gestures, "Luther."

Sam lifts his hand in a nervous wave.

"You must be exhausted." I put my arm around him. God knows, he looks like he needs some reassurance. "Come inside."

As Sam sits down on the couch, Nova joins him, and Luther goes straight to the kitchen to make coffee. I follow him, watching Nova from the other side of the cabin's open-plan living space.

"I'm sorry," Sam says, shaking his head. "I can't quite believe this." He reaches for Nova, like she's the only thing tethering him to what's real right now. "I thought I'd spend my life in that place." He searches her face. "I thought you were dead."

"I know." She presses her side against his. "I thought you were too."

"Then how did you…?"

"You'll want some coffee before you get into that," Tanner says lightly. "There's a *lot* to explain." He moves to sit opposite Nova, puts his hands on her knees, kisses her forehead while Kole stands behind the couch and strokes his large hands over her shoulders. Sam notices, but—unlike Nico—doesn't seem to find it strange that she's treating them both like her boyfriend. "Are you okay, Little Star?" Tanner asks, rubbing her outer thigh.

"I'm okay." She taps his forehead. "And you? Headache gone?"

"Good as new."

When Luther walks over with a tray of coffees, we all take one. Kole moves around the couch and sits on the other side of Nova. Luther and I remain standing.

Nova blows across the top of her coffee and closes her eyes, but when Sam reaches for his, he winces.

"You should let Tanner look at you," she says, stroking his back. To Tanner, she adds, "He was in a fight last night. He's hurt."

"I'm fine." Sam puts his coffee down on the table but breathes out sharply. "Really. I've had worse."

Nova presses her lips together as if his admission physically hurts her. "Tanner's a nurse. Please, let him look."

Tanner grins and wiggles his fingers. "I have warm hands. I'll be gentle."

A laugh bubbles in Sam's chest. "Alright," he says, "thank you."

Nova stands up and takes Sam's hand. "We'll go upstairs." She nods back at us. "We won't be long."

Tanner follows them. When they're gone, I sit next to Kole and take a long sip of coffee. "Okay, Luther. What else do we need to know? What the hell happened in that place?"

31

SAM

We're in a cabin in the woods. I don't know how far we traveled from Red Rock, but it's quieter here. So quiet. Upstairs, Nova guides me to the bed. I sit down, and she kneels in front of me.

She puts her hands on my arms. "You'll be okay now. You're with us."

I stroke the side of her face. A face I've seen in my dreams every night for twenty years. "I never thought I'd see you again."

"I know." She kisses my palm. It should probably feel strange, but it doesn't.

"Okay, Nova. My turn." Tanner helps her up, then asks me to remove my shirt.

He's a tall, good-looking guy. Light brown hair. Thick and floppy. The kind who'd be perfectly at home surfing in California or on the high school soccer team. As I peel off my gray shirt, his smile fades.

Nova lets out a small gasp.

"It's really not as bad as it looks." I stare down at my chest. Barely an inch of skin remains unblemished. "They let them settle for a few days, then heal me before the next show."

Nova closes her eyes, the image too much for her.

"Let them settle?" Tanner pulls a stool from the dressing table and sits in front of me.

"They want the scars." I swallow hard. "The people who come to the club—they like them."

Tanner's examining the bite wound on my shoulder. It's deeper than the rest. Rolo got carried away; he's not supposed to draw so much blood so quickly.

Thinking of the others, still in their cages, I shudder.

"I'll fetch my bag. I'll be back." Tanner disappears back downstairs, leaving Nova and me alone for the first time.

She takes his place on the stool. "I'm sorry," she says, her eyes reading a hundred stories etched on my skin. "I'm so sorry I didn't come sooner."

"How did you know?" I ask, sliding my hand into hers.

Nova breathes in slowly. "Do you remember a woman named Sarah?" She takes her phone from her pocket and hands it to me. On the screen, there's an image of me, Nova, and her parents.

Alice and Charles. I trace my thumb over their faces, then swipe to the next. A blond woman holding a toddler, smiling at the camera. "That's me…" The smile on the young boy's face makes my stomach constrict. "That's Sarah." I look at Nova. "I remember her. She was my nanny. After the fire, when your parents…" I trail off as memories I've kept shut away for years start to pummel my brain. "She wrote to me for a long time. Told me she was going to come for me, but she never did. Then—" I screw my eyes shut.

"You disappeared." Nova touches my elbow. "But she never stopped looking for you. A couple of days ago, she told Luther the truth. She told him you were alive." She draws herself up straighter and tries to smile. "Tanner was the one who found you. He's an empath. He can…" She trails off and shakes her head. Smiling again, she adds, "It's a lot. There's a lot to explain, and I will. But for now, you just need to know you're safe here with us. We've got you."

"And Sarah?" Emotion tugs at my chest. I can't picture her face very well, but I remember her handwriting and the stack of letters I used to keep by my bed.

"She's not here, but she's close by." Nova looks around as Tanner comes back into the room. He's holding a medical bag, which he opens on the bed.

As he cleans, stitches, and heals my wounds, Nova watches carefully. "You don't have any scars from the fire," she whispers.

I know which fire she's talking about. "Couple on my leg." I look down at my pants. "The rest weren't too bad. They fixed them at the hospital before they let me go."

She's stroking the birthmark on my wrist. "It really is you," she says quietly.

"It's me." I tweak my thumb under her chin, wincing as Tanner applies pressure to a wound on my back and mutters an incantation to relieve the pain. A yawn builds in my chest. Exhaustion creeps through me.

"You should rest." Tanner pats my shoulder and stands up. "The pain spells will make you sleepy."

"We have too much to talk about..." I reach for Nova, but she kisses my forehead and helps me lie back on the bed.

"We have all the time in the world." She strokes my face. "Rest now. I'll be here when you wake up."

32

NOVA

I stay with Sam until he wakes up. The low rumble of the guys' voices, coming up through the floorboards, is soothing. I wonder what Luther is telling them. How much detail he's giving about our trip, Madame, and the horror of the stage show.

Part of me expects the voice to come to me again. With Sam here, I'm waiting for it to tell me what happens next. My cheeks flush as I think of Kole and wonder whether we need to do something to bring on another vision. Whether he needs to taste me again, and I need to let him.

"Nova?" Sam stirs, sitting up slowly, holding his side.

"Still here," I say, folding my arms in front of my stomach because constantly holding his hands feels a bit too full-on.

A smile parts his lips. He has dark brown eyes, pale skin, and thick curly hair. He looks down at his torso and shudders.

"If you want to shower, I can show you where the bathroom is."

"Thank you." He reaches for the water on the nightstand and takes a long drink. "It's been a while since I had a hot shower."

I open my mouth to speak, but nothing comes out. There are too many questions swirling in my brain. I need to know how he ended up in that place, how Madame ended up *owning* him. What he did for them. What they did to him.

As if he can see the confusion on my face, Sam inches closer and strokes a gentle finger across my knuckles. "I want to tell you all of it," he says gently. "I want you to know my life."

"Me too." I catch his hand and stroke it. "But there's so much, I don't know where to start."

"How about we start with that shower?" he asks, making a show of sniffing his armpits. "I promise you, it's long overdue."

Downstairs, I point Sam in the direction of the bathroom. "I'll find you some fresh clothes," I tell him. "Take your time."

When he disappears, and the water starts running, the others hurry over. Tanner kisses me hard on the lips. Mack stands in front of me. "Are you alright?"

"You already asked me that," I say, smiling at him. "I'm fine. Luther took good care of me."

In his armchair by the window, Luther simply nods.

"Luther filled us in on what happened," Tanner says. "It sounds rough. You saw a lot." He fixes his gaze on mine. He can feel it, the swirling pit of emotion in my stomach.

"I've no idea what he's been through." I wrap my arms around myself. "I thought my life was hard, but Sam's must have been…" I can't find the words.

"He's safe now," Kole offers. "He's with us."

Sitting down on the edge of the couch, I glance at the whiskey bottle on the side. "Can I?" I ask. It's approaching sunset outside, so doesn't feel too early. Besides, I need something to calm me down enough so that I can think straight.

Luther pours me a glass. Tanner clicks some ice into it and hands it to me. Closing my eyes, I take a sip.

"What have you done to our girl, Luther?" Tanner quips. "Took her away to the big city. She comes back drinking whiskey?"

In response, Luther pours his own drink and stares down into it.

Kole sits down and pulls me onto his lap. He sighs quietly. His body hums with pleasure at being close to me again. I lean into him. "So, what do we do now?" I ask as Tanner sits and slings his arm onto the back of the couch, winding it around Kole.

"Now?" Luther asks. "You're the one with the visions. You tell us."

Cutting in, so I don't have to answer, Mack says, "We know something's happening in town. We can't be sure if it's to do with the League or the Bureau. So far, both of them seem to be lying low. But I don't imagine it'll stay that way for long."

"You guys are on the run?" Sam appears in the doorway of the bathroom, towel slung around his waist. His chest glistens as droplets of water follow the lattice work of scars. "Well, shit. Looks like I jumped out of the frying pan and into the fire." He smiles at me and walks over. Nodding at my whiskey he adds, "Could I?"

Luther obliges, and Sam perches on the arm of the couch next to me.

"It's a really long story," I tell him, laughing a little.

"Well, I don't think I've got to be at work tonight, seeing as you guys bought me out of my contract. So, I've got time."

Sam's light-hearted sense of humor completely surprises me. After everything he went through last night, everything he's *lived* through over the past ten years, he's still managing to seem... normal.

"What do I need to know?" he asks.

Breathing out between pursed lips, Luther turns to the window and stares out at the lake.

"I don't even know where to start," I say, looking at Tanner for help.

"I guess," Tanner says, "it starts with Kole. He's a seer. He was undercover with the League when he accessed a prophecy called The Phoenix Prophecy..."

33

NICO

We arrive at The Hollow just after midnight. The moon is full and swollen, casting eerie shadows between the trees.

The drone footage on the news didn't do justice to the damage Kole inflicted on the lawn. Centuries-old tree roots bulge up from beneath the earth, thick and twisted, like gnarled fingers reaching for the house itself. Trenches of black soil lay in their wake. Ahead, The Hollow's windows are shattered. Some are pierced by the vines that snake from the woods, over the roots, and up the stone steps. Others must have shattered by the force of the Bureau's spells when they broke the shielding spells.

As we weave between them—roots, vines, and trenches—the earth vibrates beneath us. In the trenches, it seems to be moving. Undulating. Humming with whatever power Kole unleashed.

I feel like a traitor and an intruder.

Walking amongst us, the only witch in a pack of wolves, Eve is wide-eyed with excitement. She stops, takes off her boots, and wriggles her toes into the cold, dewy grass. She sighs, stretches out her arms, and looks up at the night sky. Then she twirls in a circle, laughing.

When we reach the steps, Ragnor shifts. The others follow.

Mother stands next to him, looking up at the building. "You're sure?" she asks.

Ragnor nods. Behind them, Eve says, "Can't you feel it? Can't you *feel* the darkness?"

I'm the last to shift. Still sore and aching. It's an effort and leaves me panting. Ragnor looks me up and down. His jaw twitches in disappointment—or maybe disgust—then he turns and stalks inside. Through the kitchen, down the hall, into the lounge where Kole and Tanner took Nova the first night we were all together.

I stare at the unlit fireplace, imagining her standing in its glow. The two of them caressing her, soothing her, wiping her ex-boyfriend's blood from her body.

Ragnor snaps his eyes to the fireplace. Instantly, Eve clicks her fingers and it's lit.

"Reinforcements," he says to her. "I don't want those mages getting back in here."

"Or the Bureau," Mother adds.

Ragnor snarls at the mere mention of them.

"I'll see to it." Eve strokes his arm. I notice the pained look on my mother's face and look away.

When she's gone, Mother and I stand next to each other by the window, waiting for Ragnor to tell us what to do. The others swarm all over the house. I hear them throwing doors back on their hinges, emptying closets and drawers, and jumping on beds.

Ragnor flicks his hand at me. Like I'm a bothersome fly or a gnat he wants rid of. "Leave us," he says.

Mother's eyes narrow, but she doesn't object.

"Leave us," Ragnor repeats, his lips curling into a snarl.

I close the door behind me and go back outside. Sitting on the rim of the now-empty fountain, I look at the house. It is sad and broken without Nova inside it.

I am sad and broken too.

I'm still outside when Ragnor emerges from the house and disappears into the forest with Andre and three others.

When they return, they're carrying a coffin while Eve is dancing around them.

34

KOLE

It's early when Mack's phone rings. He sits up in bed and answers it quietly. Nova carries on sleeping, but Tanner and I wake and watch him closely. We all spent the night in bed together. No sex. I think we all just wanted to absorb the feeling of being close to her again.

When Mack hangs up, his face is gray. "That was Rev. Things are looking pretty bad in town. Riots. Looting."

"Humans? A.M.A.?" I ask.

Mack shakes his head. "She said it's like the whole place has a hex on it. Like everyone's losing their minds."

"A hex?" I inch to the edge of the bed. Tanner eases his arm from beneath Nova's head and joins me.

"She also said the Bureau's sending agents to scour the woods."

"We should reinforce the obscuring spell." Tanner springs up and grabs his clothes. "Let's wake Luther."

Downstairs, however, Luther is already awake. In fact, he looks like he hasn't slept at all. On the couch, Sam is snoring lightly. His arm is up over his head, a blanket slung over his middle, exposing a scarred chest.

Last night, after we explained the prophecy and everything that's happened since Nova arrived in Phoenix Falls, he sat back with wide eyes and simply nodded. "Okay," he said. "That makes sense."

Got to hand it to the kid, he's resilient as hell.

I nod for Luther to join us outside. When Mack explains Rev's update, Luther agrees we should check the spell. But as we stride out to the edge of the mask, he seems distracted.

When we're finished, and heading back inside, I catch Luther's arm and tug him to one side while the others return to the cabin. "Hey, man, are you okay?"

He hesitates, then leans against the nearest tree and rubs his face with his palms. "Fine. Just didn't sleep much last night."

I study his face. I move closer, my chest inches from his. I force him to meet my eyes. Something flickers in them. A darkness laced with fire. "Shit. Did you and Nova? The two of you—"

"No." Luther shakes his head. "We didn't." He puts his hand on my arm. "I swear. We didn't."

I fold my arms and wait for an explanation.

"We didn't, but would you care? If we had?"

I consider the question. Sharing her with Tanner and Mack is easy. It feels right, like it absolutely has to be that way. Watching her with them, being with the two of them while I'm with her, it's the best fucking sex I've ever had. But Luther? Does he fit? "I don't know." I shake my head. "Do you have feelings for her?"

"Would it make it okay if I did?" Luther asks. There's a sharpness to his voice, like he's furious with himself and can't figure out why.

"Yeah," I nod. "It would, but if it's just cos she looked sensational in a corset…"

Luther's eyes narrow.

"She sent us a picture. I wouldn't blame you—"

"She sent you…" Luther looks disappointed.

"You're sad you didn't get that image all to yourself?" I thump him on the shoulder, trying to lighten the mood. "Come on, man. You'll be okay. Just jerk off and get her out of your system."

"Tried that," Luther mutters. "Didn't work."

"Didn't *work*?" I look down at his crotch. He's never had that issue before.

"No, I mean, it didn't get her out of my system. It barely touched the sides." He waves his hand at the surrounding trees. "All this going on, and the only thing I can think about is her cunt on my face."

Hearing those words come from Luther's mouth, about Nova, a jolt of hunger stiffens my muscles. My eyes flash with anger. Luther notices.

"Don't…" I tell him.

"It's okay for you three to share, but not me?" Luther squares up to me. Is he trying to provoke me?

"We care for her. You care about your dick."

"Is that what you think of me? That I'm incapable of caring? Because none of you have a great track record with relationships either."

"Don't push me, Luther. Nova is different. She's our girl now. You know that."

Luther's jaw twitches. "Okay, so maybe I'll just ask her? Ask if three's enough or if she wants one more?" Luther pushes past me as if he's intent on going straight inside, finding Nova, and fucking her right this minute. "The prophecy says *five,* right?"

I grab his arm and throw him back against the tree. Sparks bloom behind him, lighting up the trunk, then fluttering into the air.

He steps forward, attempting to move around me a second time.

Again, I throw him back.

This time, he waits. Air rising and falling in his chest. I look down and see an erection straining against his pants. My dick twitches in response.

Luther and I have fucked once before. Just once. The night I left to join the League. We were drunk. It was messy. We never revisited it.

I move toward him, squaring my shoulders, drawing myself up so I'm bigger and broader and meaner than he is. He looks at me, his eyes soften. "Fuck her out of me," he says. "You do it for Tanner. You fuck the darkness away, like he takes yours."

My jaw clenches at the mention of Tanner.

"Fuck me until she's out of my head," he growls with a slight desperation in his voice.

I hesitate for just a moment then, in one swift movement, I take hold of his shoulders and spin him around. I look at the branches above us, flick my fingers, and pull two of them down to twist around Luther's wrists and hold him in place.

When his pants are down around his ankles, I unfasten my jeans and take out my dick. He pushes his ass out for me. I spit into my hands, moisten my shaft, then ease into him. I go slow, in then out, a little further each time.

"Ready?" I ask, poised for one final thrust.

"I told you to fuck her out of me." Luther slams back onto my shaft. I groan and lean back, watching my balls hit the back side of his.

As I pull him onto me, again and again, making Luther tug

against his restraints. I know what he wants, so I reach around him and wrap my fingers around his dick. I fist it in tandem with the motion of my cock, moving my palm over the metal ladder beneath his skin, creating a friction that makes him groan. As if he's on a precipice between pleasure and pain, and doesn't know which way he's going to fall, he asks desperately, "Tell me what it's like to fuck her."

"You think I'm going to tell you what my girlfriend's cunt tastes like?" I whisper in his ear.

Luther groans.

"You will never know what she tastes like." I let his wrists go, and he slams his knuckles into the tree. A lightning rod of fire shoots down into the ground. It grows hot under my feet. My balls tighten. Waves of pleasure roll through me.

"She was wet for me," Luther says, grinding back onto my dick as it stiffens inside him, pushing my tip onto his prostate and moaning at the pressure. "In the club. She wore crotchless panties. I felt her. She was wet for me."

I pull back.

Luther clenches, tries to keep me inside, but I push him off and come on his ass instead. He's trembling, desperate for me to return. Instead, I turn him around and take him by the throat. As I squeeze, restricting his airway just enough to make his head swim, he fists his own dick. Once. Twice. Three times. His body tenses, his muscles constrict. He cries out and braces his arm on my chest as he comes. "Fuck," he breathes, shivers shaking his muscles, falling back to rest against the tree, looking up into the branches. "Fuck."

I pull up my pants as he does the same. He opens his mouth to say something, but I return my hand to his throat and fix my eyes on his. "Don't talk about my girlfriend's cunt again, Luther."

Then I leave him outside and stalk back to the cabin.

35

NOVA

It's late morning when I wake. The light outside isn't the misty early-morning kind. It's brighter, warmer. For the first time in I'm not sure how many nights, I'm alone. The bed feels too large and too empty. But then Sam appears at the top of the stairs.

His hair falls over his face as he nods good morning. Brushing it back with his forearm, I notice he's carrying two steaming coffees.

"The guys are outside. They said something about reinforcing a mask?" He hands me a mug and perches next to me.

"We masked almost the entire forest," I tell him, blowing across the surface of the hot liquid. "The lake too."

"How does that work?" Sam asks. "I mean, what would people see? A big black hole?"

I frown and try to remember how Mack explained it. "I think it's a bit like creating an alternate version of what's here. So, they'll see the woods and the lake but nothing that would lead them to us. No cabin. Landmarks in the wrong place."

"They'd get lost? A bit like a labyrinth?"

"Something like that." I laugh and sip the coffee. "If I'm honest, I'm still new at this stuff."

"It's a lot." Sam tucks one leg up underneath him. He's wearing a pair of Mack's sweatpants and a loose navy tee. "Learning you're destined to save the world? That's..." he widens his eyes, "*big*."

I tilt my head to the side. "I guess so. Although, it's all happened so quickly I'm not sure I've had a chance to really take it in."

Sam chuckles. "I know that feeling. Yesterday I woke up in a cage. Today, I woke up on a big comfy couch looking out at a lake and a bunch of trees." He sighs and shakes his head. "Do you know when I last saw *trees,* Nova?"

I close my eyes. The idea of him being shut away for so long makes my chest hurt.

"It's okay." He nudges my leg with his foot. "It's a good thing. There's a whole world out there I need to experience. I'm not going to waste it feeling sorry for myself."

I study his face. His softness reminds me of Tanner, but he's got something else too; a youthfulness, an optimism I didn't expect.

"So, what's the plan today?" he asks. "Can we spend some time catching up or is there some urgent business to attend to?"

I'm about to answer him when a waft of cooking smells drifts up from the kitchen. "Pancakes," I tell him, wriggling my eyebrows. "Before anything else... pancakes."

Downstairs, Kole is cooking while Mack, Tanner, and Luther stare at a large map of the woods. The table is set with plates, glasses, a pot of coffee, and a jug of juice. It reminds me of the very first morning I met them all, except now there's one more.

Sam greets the guys with handshakes and patting of backs. It's different with him than with Nico. They distrusted Nico from the second they laid eyes on him. With Sam, it's like he fits right in. As if he was always supposed to be here.

While Luther points at something and Mack nods, Tanner checks Sam's wounds. "Looking good," he says.

Their eyes catch... or was I imagining it?

We sit down and, for a while, talk about nothing important. The guys make fun of Mack, explaining he's the daddy of the group —and that he sometimes turns into a polar bear. They tell Sam that Luther built the cabin with his own bare hands, and that back in town both Mack and Luther were cops. Then, finally, chatter descends into something more serious.

"Now that Sam's here, we need to decide what we do next." Luther pushes his plate away and places his palms on the table. "We think the Bureau has started to scour the woods. So far, they haven't got close to the cabin, but we can't hang around much longer. We need a plan." He hesitates then adds, "So, does anyone have any suggestions?"

"We need the Bureau on our side." Mack strokes his beard. "I still believe that."

"Why?" Tanner asks, a little sharply. "They haven't helped so far. In fact, they seem determined to do the opposite of helping. Shouldn't we be focussed on what Ragnor's next move is?"

At the mention of Ragnor's name, a shiver creeps up my spine.

"He's trying to prevent the prophecy. He *wants* the underworld to rise." Tanner is thinking out loud, waving his hand as if it will help his brain to work faster. "He must be close to whatever he's planning on doing to unleash it. Otherwise, Nova wouldn't have set fire to her apartment."

My forehead creases as I try to work out what he means.

Darkly, Kole says, "Something triggered the prophecy. Your power has been dormant for ten years. If Ragnor wasn't close, none of this would have happened."

"Raising the underworld?" Sam asks, almost laughing. "Is that actually possible? I mean, the occasional demon has come through *Spine* over the years. But it takes a heck of a lot of dark magick to capture one. How much would H.E.L. need to set the entirety of the nether realms free?"

"A lot." Kole inhales deeply. His jaw twitches. "They'd need a lot."

"Maybe I'll have another vision." I tap my temple with my index finger. "A vision that'll tell us what to do next."

"I don't think we can afford to sit around and wait for that to happen," snaps Luther. "I say we divide forces. Mack and I tackle the Bureau. Get Nova's test results to Annalise. If she sees them, if we can *speak* to her face-to-face, she'll help us." He taps the map. "Kole and Tanner go into town. Be discreet. Find out what the heck is going on, because if Phoenix Falls is the center of all this—and folk have started acting strangely—I'm willing to bet dark magick is floating around somewhere."

I'm about to object to the idea of Kole and Tanner going into town alone, risking being caught, when Sam says, "Nova and I? What do we do?"

"You two are on research." Luther folds his arms.

"Research?" I narrow my eyes at him.

"Search every archive, every copy of every ancient text. Look for something that might indicate when this uprising is supposed to happen." Luther looks at Mack for help.

"Most archives are online," Mack says. "We've searched them before, but not having the slightest clue when the prophecy would start, it was almost impossible to narrow them down. Now we have a year and a month, we know the planetary alignment. That'll help." He meets my eyes, sensing I'm about to break out in hives at the idea of trying to dissect a bunch of ancient academic texts. "I'll get you started," he says softly. "You'll soon get the hang of it."

"If you say so," I reply, smiling nervously.

For the rest of the day, Mack helps Sam and I get to grips with various clunky online archives. The search functions are dreadful and accessing them via the old laptop Luther pulled out of an upstairs closet is not easy.

While we work, Kole and Tanner scour the news for signs of what's been happening in town, and Luther researches Annalise McCourt—desperately trying to find a way to contact her without going through the official channels.

By the time evening rolls around, we're all tired, hungry, and square-eyed from staring at our respective devices.

Kole and Tanner have decided it will be best to leave early; sneak out before sunrise and take the back alleyways to get to Rev's. But Luther is no closer to finding a way to contact Annalise, and nothing that seems relevant has come up in our archive searches either.

Putting the laptop aside, I offer to make dinner. Sam watches me while I boil pasta and throw in a jar of pre-made sauce. "I feel like I missed a big part of growing up," he says. "Learning how to be an adult." He swipes his fingers through his hair. "I have no idea how to cook, or clean, or…" He stops. Color flushes his cheeks.

Remembering what Madame said about him—that he's never had sex before—my cheeks pink too. "Don't worry," I say loudly, "Luther can't cook either."

We eat together, gathered around the table, Sam next to me. He has a huge appetite, bigger even than Kole's, and polishes off three large portions. Being near him feels easy. As if we've been this way forever.

Yet, it also feels different from how I expected it to feel. He's my foster-brother, but when he moves, laughs, or smiles, I find myself looking at him in a way I'm sure I wouldn't contemplate if we'd spent our lives as siblings. And, more than once, I'm certain he looks at me too.

As guilt and confusion tug at my stomach, I try to push it to one side.

While we start mulling over what to do tomorrow, I feel something brush my leg. I look up to see Tanner wiggling his eyebrows at me from across the table.

As I play footsie with him back, Luther clears the dishes and Sam asks whether anyone minds if he takes a walk outside.

"It's been a long time since I saw the moon at night," he says, glancing toward the dark sky above the lake.

"Go for it, man." Tanner pats his shoulder. "We'll see you later."

I'm drying dishes next to Luther when Tanner wraps his arms around my waist and nibbles my ear. "Leave those," he says. "I need to show you how much I missed you." He tugs my hand and tries to pull me toward the stairs.

I bat him away playfully and shake my head. "Mack's up there making a phone call."

"I'm sure he won't mind an interruption." Tanner tugs me to him and pushes his hips so they jut up against mine. I glance back at Luther. He's not looking at us, still hunched over the sink. Tanner runs a finger down my spine and raises his eyebrows at me in anticipation.

Finally, I can't hold back any longer. I toss the dishcloth onto the counter and follow him upstairs.

36

LUTHER

K ole emerges from the bathroom freshly showered. His eyes flick to the whiskey bottle and the glass in my hand.

"Not joining the party?" I ask him, raising my eyes to the ceiling. Nova, Tanner, and Mack are up there. Laugher and hell-knows-what-else noises have been coming down through the floor for the past fifteen minutes.

"Not sure I can be trusted." Kole runs his tongue over his teeth. "I'm still…" He flexes his shoulders and tilts his head from side to side. "Amped."

"From her blood?" I ask quietly.

Kole nods and sits next to me on the couch.

I look down into my whiskey. "Listen, Kole, I'm sorry about before. I shouldn't have talked about Nova like that. I just needed..." I trail off. I don't know how to explain what I needed. Release? Pleasure? Pain? I have no idea.

Kole's lips twitch into something that's almost a smile. "Did it help?"

I laugh and take a long sip of whiskey. "Will it hurt your ego if I say no?"

"Nah. I can handle it." Kole thumps me on the shoulder.

"Did you tell Nova?"

"Yes."

"Did she mind?"

Kole shakes his head. "No, she didn't mind. She was surprised, but she didn't mind."

"Did you tell her that I..."

"I said it was a *heat* of the moment thing." Kole's trying to lighten the mood, but I can't muster a smile. After a pause, he says, "Listen, Luther..."

I reach for the whiskey bottle on the coffee table and top up my glass.

"If you have feelings for Nova, true feelings, don't fight it." He smooths his hand over his beard. "You don't have to be alone, you know."

"I'm not alone. I have my brothers," I tell him.

Kole breathes in heavily, then sighs. "If it was just sex, what we did out there would have helped." He tilts his head. "But what you're feeling? It's not just lust, is it? It's different." He fixes his eyes on mine. "When I'm not with her, it's like my whole body is on the verge of imploding. Every minute I'm apart from her is a minute too long. She fills my thoughts, my veins, my dreams. She's—"

"You love her," I say bluntly. "That's what love is like, or so I'm told."

Kole hesitates. "It's more than that. Bigger than that."

"The prophecy," I say, taking another drink of whiskey. "You're destined to be with her. Whatever's coming, you're wrapped up in it. You've known that since this all started, way before you even met her. You're bonded to her, the three of you." Looking at Sam, sitting cross-legged outside, staring up at the stars, thinking of the way he and Nova look at each other—far from the way siblings should look at one another—I add, "Maybe the four of you."

"Fated to *five*." Kole picks up the whiskey bottle and takes a long swig. He looks at me sideways. "Like you said. The prophecy says *five*, Luther. What makes you think you're not part of that?"

I close my eyes and take another sip of whiskey. When I open them, Sam is back inside, crossing the room. "Nova upstairs?" he asks.

Kole nods.

"Shall we tell him to stay here?" I ask quietly, flicking my eyes toward the stairs as Sam trots up them.

Kole smirks a little. "No," he says, sitting back. "Let him go to her."

37

TANNER

"I ...I'm sorry. I'll go," Sam stammers, lingering in the doorway. I turn around and instantly notice the arousal pushing against his pants. Nova closes her thighs, still leaning on Mack's chest.

"Wait." I hop down from the bed and cross the room. "You should stay."

Sam braces a hand on the doorframe. "She's..." he shakes his head. "She's my sister."

"Does she feel like your sister?" I ask, meeting his eyes. "Or does the connection you have with her feel like something else? You two have something—I won't deny that—but you were only in the same house for twelve months as her foster brother. So, maybe it's something else..."

He swallows hard. Lust drips from his body. It swirls around him, vibrating so hard it's overwhelming. He loves Nova, but not like a sister. She's his, like she is ours. It's the same way Kole feels, the way Mack feels, the way I feel. He needs her.

I look over my shoulder. Nova is watching us. She needs him, too. It's been obvious since the moment they walked into the cabin together.

"You're an empath?" Sam says, studying my face.

I nod.

His lips twitch with embarrassment. "So, you know..."

"I know the last thing you want to do right now is leave this room." I tweak my head toward the bed. "Ask her. If you're scared, ask her."

Sam hesitates for a moment, then strides forward. "Nova?"

She sits up, pulling away from Mack while he watches her. "Don't go." She smiles, meeting Sam's gaze. "Please, don't go."

Standing behind him, I slide my hands under Sam's tee and push it up over his shoulders. Old and new scars pepper his skin. Silver slashes, purple grooves. I step around him and sit back down on the bed. "You haven't done this before, have you?" I ask.

Sam shakes his head.

How a guy with a body like that can still be a virgin, I have no idea. But the thought of all the things he's about to feel and discover sends a wave of arousal to my dick. "Then come here and let me show you what she likes."

As I speak, Nova releases a small mewing sound and lies back on Mack's chest again. He strokes her hair, runs gentle fingers down her throat, caresses her breasts through her shirt.

Sam is standing next to the bed. "Kiss her," I tell him. He sits down at her side. Slowly, he leans over her. He gazes into her eyes. She closes them as he brushes his lips against hers, hesitant at first then bolder. Searching. He runs his tongue along her lower lip. She pushes her fingers through his hair. At the same time, Mack nuzzles her neck.

They kiss for a long time. Nova arches her back and presses her body against Sam's chest. His back ripples as her hands skim his scars. She moans into his mouth, then says, "Tanner, don't stop…"

Not needing to be told twice, I crawl up to the other side of her. I tell Sam to kiss her throat. He obeys. As his tongue teases her skin, I slip my hand under Nova's shirt and draw small delicate circles on her stomach.

Behind her, Mack eases her up and pulls her shirt over her head.

"Here," he tells Sam, bringing his hand to Nova's black lacy bra. "See if you can feel her nipples through the fabric."

As Nova lies back down, wriggling into Mack, Sam smooths his thumbs over her breasts.

"Can you feel them?" I ask.

He nods. "Yes."

"Do you want to touch them?" Mack traces his fingers across Nova's chest.

"Yes."

"Slide the straps over her shoulders," Mack tells him. As Sam does what he's told, Mack says, "Good boy."

Nova groans and closes her eyes. Instantly, my dick is rock hard. I tug my pants down and take my length in my hand, but then realize Nova is reaching for me. I move closer so she can wrap her fingers around me. Expertly, she runs her thumb over my slit, gathers the pre-cum then sucks it into her mouth.

Sam's eyes widen. He's watching her tongue swirl around the tip of her thumb, but then he remembers her bra. Reaching around her back, his hands grazing Mack's chest, he fumbles to unclip it. When he finally succeeds, he laughs and shakes his head. "We'll practice that one," Nova says, sweeping her bra to the floor before returning her hand to my cock.

Now that her breasts are exposed, Sam stares at her. "Fuck," he breathes.

Mack cups them for her, taking their weight in his palms. He looks at me. "Why don't you show Sam how she likes her nipples to be sucked?"

I grin eagerly and pepper her stomach with kisses as I make my way up her body. When I reach her breasts, I look at Sam and wait for him to position himself next to me. Nova looks at us both, mouths poised to take a nipple each. Her eyes roll back as she breathes, "Holy hell."

Slowly, deliberately, I make a circle with my tongue. Then I close my mouth and suck, keeping the pressure, tweaking her between my teeth, then lapping until she cries out.

As Mack moves his fingers over her wet breasts, taking the place of our tongues, Sam and I sit back. I look over at him. His dick is so hard, his pants look like they might split open.

Nova tilts her head back. "Kiss me, Daddy." She pulls Mack toward her. He kisses her upside down, holding her face still as his mouth hungrily devours hers.

"Fuck," Sam breathes again.

I tug his hand, pull him to the bottom of the bed, then ease Nova's legs open for us. "You know where her clitoris is?" I ask.

Sam swallows hard and nods.

"Show me," I tell him.

With his index finger, he points to the swollen, wet bud.

"Okay, seriously," Nova says, looking down at us, her entire body flushed with arousal. "One of you needs to touch me."

"Show me." Sam looks at me. His eyes catch mine. Oh, I get it. He doesn't just like touching Nova; he likes watching *me* touch her too.

Smiling, I begin to massage her clit. I play with it until her hips match my rhythm, then I use my tongue instead, nibbling at her pussy, savoring every taste.

"Your turn," I say, forcing myself to stop.

Sam mirrors me exactly. While Nova begins to pant and groan, he uses his fingers and tongue like an expert.

"Fuck me," she pleads. "Somebody, fuck me."

"Do you want to?" I ask. "'Cause, I get it if you want your first time to be a little more... private."

He shakes his head and swipes his fingers through his thick, curly hair. "You expect me to walk away from this?"

I smile and nod, then put my hands on his hips and move him into position. He leans down and kisses her. Nova loops her arms around his neck while Mack continues to play with her breasts. When Sam takes his mouth away from hers, she strokes the side of his face. "You're sure?"

"I'm sure." He looks back at me. I'm behind him. I grip his impressive length and grin at Nova over Sam's shoulder. "Lucky girl," I tell her. Noticing where my hand is, she moans and opens her legs wider.

I guide Sam to her entrance. "Just the tip..." I let go as he eases the head of his dick into her. He shudders and breathes out hard. "Good boy. Now a little more." He moves his hips forward and sinks deeper. As Nova sighs and Mack strokes her face, Sam starts to thrust.

I move to the side so I can watch him fucking her. Nova reaches for my dick. She's lying down and has taken Mack's balls in her mouth, hungrily sucking them while he kneels over her from behind her head.

Sam picks up his pace, but then his eyes widen. He's going to come.

I let go of my own dick and reach for Sam's. He stares at me as I grip him hard, right where the tip meets the shaft. "When you feel like it's gone, I'll let go."

Sam pants heavily. I keep hold of him, squeezing the orgasm back inside him.

Finally, he nods. His eyes move to my lips. I glance at Nova. She's watching us with wide, sparkling eyes. I turn back to Sam and guide his hand to my cock. His fingers curl around me at the same time his mouth meets mine. While he fists my shaft, he eases his own back into Nova. Then he takes his hand away from me and grabs her hips, making circular movements that take her breath away as Mack massages her clit. Dancer's moves, if ever I saw them.

She arches her back. Her body stiffens. Her cheeks are flushed bright pink, and she's gripping the sheets between her hands. Sam falls forward and laces his fingers with hers as Mack slides out of the way and stands next to the bed.

We watch as Sam's orgasm thunders through him. Nova is close to coming. So close. Sam trembles on top of her. She strokes his back, while kissing his neck. When he rolls onto his side and kisses her shoulder, I dive between her legs. His cum mingles with hers. I put my fingers inside her and hook them forward. I've barely started sucking her clit when she sparks. Waves of heat shake the air. She reaches for Sam and kisses him, then kisses Mack, humming into their mouths.

Mack comes on her stomach, growling loudly and running his hands through his hair, then massaging his warm cum into her skin.

"Tanner..." Nova looks up at me. "Inside." She pulls my dick toward her. I slide in, groaning at her wetness. She clenches around me, and I let go. I come hard, the orgasm lasting a long time. When it fades, I rest my head between her breasts. Mack curls himself around her. She kisses us, strokes us, soothes us.

We fall asleep in a tangle of arms and legs, fused together. Little Star in our middle.

38

NICO

E ve is standing in front of the fountain. Moonlight illuminates her face, making her skin paler and the black lines at the corners of her eyes darker. She takes a vial of FHB from her long black robe and swallows it down in one gulp. She licks her lips, staining them a dark nauseating red, then runs her tongue over her teeth.

"You're certain?" Ragnor asks her. "This is the place?"

"Can't you *feel* it?" she asks, swaying back and forth. "It's beneath us. His power. Can't you *feel* it?"

Clearly, my father can't feel anything. His jaw twitches. He turns to the pack, standing like soldiers behind us, waiting for their orders. "Andre," he snaps. "Now."

Immediately, Andre scurries back to the house. Three others follow him.

When they emerge again at the top of the steps, they're carrying the coffin.

A violent shudder grips my spine. Despite the fact we're in public, and next to Ragnor, Mother reaches for my hand. Her palm is clammy. She closes her eyes as the coffin approaches.

"What's in there?" I ask, dread settling in my stomach.

She doesn't answer me, just closes her eyes.

Gently, Andre and the others lower the coffin to the ground. Ragnor nods at them. "Go," he says. "Back inside. All of you."

Mother starts to walk away too, but Ragnor catches her by the wrist. "You'll stay, Kayla," he barks at her. "Your son too."

Usually, when he speaks to her like this, I see fire in her eyes. But at this moment, I see pain and fear. Mother lowers her head, licks her lips in submission, then slots her hands together behind her back and stands stock still. Watching.

I move to stand beside her. I can smell the fear coming off her now. In waves. But Ragnor and Eve aren't afraid. They're excited.

Eve kneels and smooths her hands over the coffin lid. She presses her cheek to it. "Not long," she whispers. "You'll be back with us soon, and what a sight it will be."

"Ragnor." Mother's voice is a deep growl. "It's not too late to change your mind."

He doesn't look at her. He's kneeling on the other side of the coffin. "You are a spectator, Kayla. That is all."

I try to meet her gaze, to tell her it's not too late for us either; we could run. Right now, we could run away from him and this place and never return. But she simply stares vacantly ahead, as if what's about to happen is now inevitable.

When Ragnor pries open the coffin lid, the stench of death fills the air. It congeals in my throat. I gag and throw my hand over my mouth. Mother coughs and looks away.

But Eve is smiling. "There she is. Hello, my pretty."

Ragnor's face has changed. He's smiling. Gently, like he's picking up an infant from a crib, he reaches into the coffin. When he sits back up, a woman is cradled in his arms.

A dead woman.

Thick, gnarled skin stretched tight over her bones. Sunken cheeks, flesh eaten away, gaping open, exposing white flashes of bone beneath. Thin hair, wiry, black.

A little more than a skeleton, but a lot less than a person. She is an unmoving zombie.

"Elena," Ragnor breathes, stroking his index finger down the *thing's* face.

A small mewing sound escapes Mother's lips. She looks as if she is about to vomit.

"It's time, my sweet. Time for you to return to me." He kisses her forehead. As his lips press against her rotting flesh, a swirling mass of dread and fear rushes through my veins. "I did what he asked. I found the Phoenix. I did it for you, my darling. I did it so you can come home. So you can come back to me."

Mother lets out a sob. It wracks her chest. She arches her back and clutches her stomach.

Eve claps her hands. "I'm so terribly excited," she coos.

"What now?" Ragnor asks, his features sharpening as he looks up at Eve.

"Now," Eve says softly, "we call the King to Earth." She reaches over and places one hand on Elena's chest, the other on Ragnor's. "We give him the Phoenix. He brings your love back to you, and together," she says, eye alight, "we raise the underworld."

*Thank you for reading **The Phoenix Prophecy, Book Three: Ashes**. I'm sorry to leave you on a cliffhanger but Book Four is available now!*
You can grab it here.

If you'd like to read Sam's first time from Sam and Nova's POVs, head over to my Facebook Group and let me know.

To stay up to date with special print editions and audiobooks, sign up to my newsletter.

And, as always, if you enjoyed reading Ashes, please consider leaving a review on Amazon, Goodreads, or TikTok.

END OF ASHES
THE PHOENIX PROPHECY BOOK THREE

Book One, Nova, July 2022

Book Two, Blaze, August 2022

Book Three, Ashes, September 2022

Book Four, Embers, October 2022

Book Five, Flames, 16th December 2022

Book Six, Fire Bird, 16th January 2023

LOVE ASHES?

If you enjoyed Ashes, I would be incredibly grateful if you'd leave a review so that others can discover it too!

As an independent author, reviews are one of the most important tools we have to help spread the word about our books.

Even if it's short, it will be *hugely* appreciated.

Simply visit Amazon, search for The Phoenix Prophecy and hit 'leave a review'.

ABOUT CARA

If you love why-choose romance, magic, super-hot mages, and even hotter RH scenes, then we're destined to be friends.

I mean it when I say I love keeping in touch with my readers. So, come say hi in my Facebook group, on TikTok, or follow me on Amazon for updates.

I'll also be launching a direct store on my website very soon, for special edition print, audio and merch. So, *sign up to my newsletter* to stay tuned.

www.caraclare.com

P.S. There has been a lot of discussion in the book community recently about removing the term 'RH' and referring to the genre as why-choose instead. I'd like to assure readers I'm working on making this change throughout my catalog but it will take time for the algorithms of various platforms - as well as reader awareness - to catch up. Therefore, you may still see the term Reverse Harem alongside why-choose for a short period.

amazon.com/Cara-Clare/e/B09ZQRV4QG

tiktok.com/@caraclareauthor

instagram.com/caraclareauthor

TRIGGER WARNINGS

Please scan the QR code above to access the full list of trigger warnings for this book or visit the author's website cara clare.com.

Made in the USA
Las Vegas, NV
01 October 2023

78456900R00163